Ginger bread

Rachel Cohn

Simon Pulse

New York   London   Toronto   Sydney   Singapore

For Daina and Rob

Acknowledgments

Many thanks for their support and encouragement to Steve Malk, David Gale, John Rudolph, Daina Chiu, Rob Coffman, Stephanie Gillis, Maura Brown, Wendy Zarganis, Elizabeth Bryer, Irving and Lenore Cohn, Elizabeth Cohn, Steven Merrill and Shelagh Sayers, Marcy and James Silliman, and Angelo and Mary Lee Russo.

First Simon Pulse edition June 2003

SIMON PULSE
An imprint of Simon & Schuster Children's Publishing Division
1230 Avenue of the Americas
New York, NY 10020

Also available in a Simon & Schuster Books for Young Readers hardcover edition.
Designed by Anahid Hamparian
The text of this book was set in 11-point Caxton.

Printed in the United States of America
10 9

The Library of Congress has cataloged the hardcover edition as follows:
Cohn, Rachel.
Gingerbread / by Rachel Cohn.
p. cm.
Summary: After she is expelled from a fancy boarding school, Cyd Charisse finds that her problems with her mother escalate after Cyd falls in love with a sensitive surfer and is subsequently sent from San Francisco to New York City to spend time with her biological father.
ISBN 0-689-84337-2 (hc)
[1. Mothers and daughters—Fiction. 2. Stepfamilies—Fiction. 3. Interpersonal relationships—Fiction. 4. Abortion—Fiction.] I. Title.
PZ7.C6665 Gi 2002
[Fic]—dc21   00-52225
ISBN 0-689-86020-X (Simon Pulse pbk.)

One

My so-called parents hate my boyfriend, Shrimp. I'm not sure they even believe he is my boyfriend. They take one look at his five-foot-five, surfer-shirt-wearin', baggy-jeans-slouchin', Pop Tart–eatin', spiked-hair-head self and you can just see confusion firebombs exploding in their heads, like they are thinking, Oh no, Cyd Charisse, that young man is not your homes.

Dig this: He is.

At least Shrimp always remembers to call my mother "Mrs." instead of just grunting in her direction, like most guys my age do. And no parent could deny that hanging out with Shrimp is an improvement over Justin, my ex, from my old prep school. Justin got me into trouble, big time. I'm so over the Justin stage.

Not like Sid and Nancy care much. I have done my parents the favor of becoming more or less invisible.

Sid, my father, calls me a "recovering hellion." Sid's actually my stepfather. You could say I hardly know my real father. I met him at an airport once when I was five. He was tall and skinny and had ink black hair, like me. We ate lunch in a smoky pub at the Dallas–Fort Worth airport. I did not like my hamburger so my real dad opened his briefcase and offered me a piece of homemade gingerbread he had wrapped in tinfoil.

He bought me a brown rag doll at the airport gift shop.

The cashier had made the doll herself. She said she had kept the doll hidden under her cash register waiting for just the right little girl. My real dad gave the cashier a one-hundred-dollar bill and told her to keep the change. I named my dolly Gingerbread.

Nancy and I were on our way to San Francisco to become Sid's family. My real dad was on his way back to New York, to his real wife and family. They don't know about me.

I'm fairly sure that my real dad's wife would not mind that I make scissors cuts on my arms and then pick the scabs. His real wife probably makes fresh gingerbread every day and writes Things To Do lists and does her own grocery shopping instead of having a housekeeper and a driver do everything for her, like Nancy does.

Nancy only met Justin once, at the expulsion hearing. The headmaster told her Justin and I were caught fooling around in a room loaded with Jack Daniels and prescription bottles. *In flagrante delicto* were the words the headmaster used. I failed Latin.

Nancy said Justin was from a "wonderful Connecticut family" and how could I shame her and Sid like that. It was Justin who was selling the ecstasy out of his dorm room, not me. It was Justin who said he pulled out in time. Sid and Nancy never knew about that part.

Nancy came into my room one night after I returned home to San Francisco. Sid and my younger half-sibs were at Father's Night at their French immersion school. "I hope your friends use condoms," Nancy said, which was funny because she knows Shrimp is my only friend. She threw a box of Trojans onto the lace-trimmed four-poster bed that I hate. Shrimp is a safety boy, he takes care of those things. If it had been Shrimp back in boarding school, he would have come with me to the clinic.

"Can I have a futon on the floor instead of this stupid princess bed?" I said. The thought of my mother even knowing about contraception, much less doling it out, was beyond comprehension, much less discussion.

Nancy sighed. Sighing is what she does instead of eating. "I paid ten thousand dollars to redecorate this room while you were at boarding school. No, you may not, Cyd Charisse."

Everybody in my family calls me by my first and middle name since my dad's name is pronounced the same as my first name. When she was twenty years old and pregnant with me, Nancy thought she would eventually marry my real dad. She named me after this dancer-actress from like a million years ago who starred in this movie that Nancy and real-dad saw on their first date, before she found out he had a whole other life. The real Cyd Charisse is like this incredibly beautiful sex goddess. I am okay looking. I could never be superhuman sexy like the real Cyd Charisse. I mean there is only room for so much grace and beauty in one person named Cyd Charisse, not two.

Nancy fished a pack of Butter Rum LifeSavers out of her designer jacket and held them out to me. "Want a piece of my dinner?"

Two

I might not have fallen for Shrimp if it hadn't been for Sugar Pie.

He was walking by Sugar Pie's room at the nursing home, singing this song, something about take the A train somewhere. From the pictures by Sugar Pie's bed, you could tell Shrimp might be about the same height as her long-dead twin sister, who also had short brown hair and a way of slouching. But Sugar Pie can't see so well, so I guess it was the song that made her perk up.

"Honey, is that you?" Sugar Pie called out. Sugar Pie cannot see for squat, but she's got ears stretching all the way from San Francisco back to her home state of Mississippi. She was so distracted by Shrimp's song that she laid her cards on the food tray so I could see that in the next hand she would have gin if I gave up my king of hearts, as I was about to do.

"Honey Pie?" Sugar Pie called out. Little tears snaked through the crevices of her wrinkled face.

Honey Pie was supposed to be the maid of honor at Sugar Pie's wedding to a serviceman Sugar Pie had met in Biloxi, back during World War II. But Honey Pie and the groom ran off together and eloped, and two days later, they were dead. Drove right over a cliff in Nevada when the parking brake disengaged while they were in the backseat getting wild under the shooting stars.

Sugar Pie doesn't hold grudges. She never found

another husband, but she did have a dog, a chocolate Lab she called "Honey," who was her best friend. Honey the dog died right before Sugar Pie came to live in the nursing home. That's when I became her family. At first, I only came because community service was part of the judge's orders after my little shoplifting problem, but now I come because I love Sugar.

Shrimp stood at the door to Sugar Pie's room. "Pie? Did someone say pie?" He pulled a Hostess lemon pie out of his backpack and offered it to Sugar. Sugar Pie shook her head, spraying faint tears onto my arm. I have never known Sugar Pie to turn down a sweet. I gave her my king of hearts even though as a rule I never let anyone at the home win at cards just because they are old.

Shrimp checked me out and said, "Hey, you go to my school." He had this wicked deep, gravelly voice, which you would not expect from someone so short and scrawny, and he had short brown hair with a patch of spiked platinum blond at the front towering over his forehead. If I had been a cartoon character, you would have seen the letters L-U-S-T pop into my eyes like the *ding-ding-ding* display on a Las Vegas slot machine.

Since being kicked out of the fancy boarding school in New England, I'd been attending an "alternative" high school for the arts in San Francisco. The school is really just a dumping ground for rich parents' kids who aren't total social misfits but who also have no interest in being trend victim poster children, but it's also a haven for scholarship students with actual talent, like Shrimp.

Sugar eyed Shrimp's spiked hair and deep blue eyes. "Cyd Charisse, there's your star," Sugar Pie said. She was a psychic and tarot-card reader with her own offices before she retired.

The Honey Pie blues had made Sugar Pie sleepy. She reached for a roll of quarters tucked under her mattress. "You two go have coffee on me," she said. We didn't take her money, but we took her suggestion.

Three half-caff mochiatos later, Shrimp was my main man. He was the first and only friend my age I made since returning home from New England.

He told me his nursing home community service was probation for making a midnight excursion to an expensive yuppie fitness club in the Marina and graffiti-painting a mural on the club's outside brick wall that pictured a sweaty pig with dollar bill signs for eyes. When he asked how I landed before a judge, I told him about my former habit of shoplifting from surgical supply stores.

Shrimp drew a picture of me picking a scab on the side of my thigh. He drew my skirt much shorter than it actually is, but he did capture my long legs and combat boots perfectly. I am totally flat-chested, but in the legs department, I am very blessed.

I did not care that I was five inches taller than Shrimp—more when I wear my rockin' five-inch platforms—or that he listened to disco music in a beat-up old Pinto handed down to him by his older brother. I was suffering Post-Traumatic Justin Syndrome, and Shrimp was just what I needed.

He is all heart.

Three

One day I am going to have my own commune in like Tahiti or somewhere. Not one of those psycho deals where people have to be deprogrammed afterward, but like a giant hut made of straw and purple clay. Artists and runaways and musicians will come and paint their faces and dance like they are tribal warriors. Our uniforms will be grass skirts and shirts made from flowers. Dolphins will let us ride on their backs and we won't exploit them by making bullshit movies about them later.

Shrimp and I will have our own room and we will sleep in a sleeping bag made from native plants. We will figure out how to cultivate that stuff. Gingerbread will have her own doll house under a sea breeze window in our room. We will send her outside to play when we want to fool around.

Sugar Pie will have her own special room at our commune. It will be facing the ocean. We won't be mad when she tells us to be quiet because her stories are on. We'll have a giant satellite dish nestled on a volcanic mountaintop with the words "Sugar Pie" graffiti-painted on it just for her.

Sid and Nancy and their children will visit on the holidays and pronounce our commune "darling." We won't mind when Nancy rearranges the furniture we've built ourselves. We can move it all back when she leaves.

We'll even let my real dad come and stay whenever he needs to escape the bright lights and big city and take a break from the old wife and kids. Shrimp, Sugar Pie, and I will wait on the beach for his boat to appear on the horizon. When he steps off the plank of his boat, we will have made piping hot gingerbread for him. He might just stay forever.

Four

Shrimp lives with his older brother, Wallace. They live in a cottage with sand dollars painted on the roof on this street that runs along Ocean Beach. They have a telescope on the roof.

Wallace and Shrimp are surfers. Not like those "Hey dude, I'm gonna go catch some rays and ride me some curls, heh-heh" surfers, but like broody surfers. You would have to be antipep to want to surf in fog and freezing water, surrounded by signs warning how many people die in the mean tide at Ocean Beach. If Wallace and Shrimp could spend all their time surfing, painting, and drinking coffee, they would be very happy brooding people.

Justin would not know what to do with a surfboard if you shoved one up his lacrosse-playing, brie-fed WASP ass.

Wallace is famous in Ocean Beach. Besides the fact that he's a major babe in that mysterious unattainable older guy way, Wallace is also like a neighborhood mogul. Everybody knows him as "Java the Hut." He turned a geekmeister coffee cart he pushed around in college into three coffeehouses. They are called "Java the Hut" and all three are within the Sunset District neighborhood where Ocean Beach is. People in this city care very much about their coffee, and they are also way into locally owned this, independently operated that, so Java the Hut totally rides the anti-Starbucks wave.

In New England, you could not get a decent cuppa joe except at Dunkin' Donuts. That is the one place I miss most from back East. If I could only eat Dunkin' Donuts for every meal from now until the day I died, that would be tiddley-wink with me. Instead, I survive on burritos from the Mission, potstickers from Clement Street, *yo quiero* Taco Bell from anywhere, and Shrimp's brown sugar Pop Tarts. Nancy says I will get acne from the junk I eat. She wishes she could eat what I eat.

Justin was always stoned, but he never had munchie provisions. He always made me sneak off to 7-Eleven for Doritos and Ring Dings. I was a whore for popularity then, so I would slip past the resident advisor and scale the fences at the end of the school grounds. I would come back all cold and shivering and like, "Whoo hoo, how spectaculi-cious am I, I shoplifted some extra Fireballs." Everybody in Justin's room would be like, your girlfriend is so cool, man.

I am so relieved not to be that person anymore.

Shrimp wants to know how come Rice Krispies and Cap'n Crunch and Frosted Flakes have their own mascots, but Pop Tarts doesn't. Shrimp is convinced there is some kind of conspiracy involved. He is always drawing Pop Tart mascots and sending them in to the Pop Tart company. They write polite letters back with cereal coupons enclosed. They always spell his last name wrong.

Justin was captain of the lacrosse team. I dug on his bulky biceps and tight calves. I was hormonally challenged then. Girls swooned over him and worshiped me for having him. Shallow girl, thy name was Cyd Charisse.

Until Shrimp, I didn't know it was possible to care so much for another person that your heart just wants to com-bust with happiness every time you are around that person. I think I would have wanted to die from loneliness if he and

Sugar Pie hadn't come into my life when they did. Thank you, juvenile court.

I am going to get a tattoo on my inner thigh just for Shrimp. A dancing Pop Tart logo. I'll call my mascot "Mr. Mmm-mmm good" or something. I will wear skirts so short that Nancy will think she sees something there, but she will be too afraid to ask. There are a lot of questions to which Nancy doesn't want answers. See, I failed Latin, but I still know not to dangle prepositions. In English.

I wish I could live at Wallace and Shrimp's house. They have painted murals on the walls and a pirate flag hanging on the porch and old, beat-up furniture that would make Nancy's interior decorator's facelift split open like in a horror movie. They are always listening to rickety old blues music about some crazysexy woman's cheatin' heart.

They love hanging out together. It's hard to imagine a Wallace without a Shrimp, and vice versa. I cannot imagine anyone in my family feeling that way about me.

Wallace says he would rather be walking the earth instead of brewing coffee. Wallace is embarrassed by his success, but secretly he loves being known as Java the Hut. He has to work a lot of hours. Wallace's business seriously cramps his surfing time.

Now that Shrimp has finished his community service, he is going to work at a Java the Hut store. He will still visit Sugar Pie and the rest of the folks at the home because they have the coolest faces to draw and the best stories about the "good ole days." Shrimp and I like to listen to their stories and when we leave we talk about how the "good ole days" also were about Jim Crow laws, segregation, and fascism. But we admit we could groove on swing dancing, Coca-Cola for a nickel, and not worrying about leaving your doors unlocked.

Wallace and Shrimp's parents live "abroad," as Nancy would say. They retired from their teaching jobs and joined the Peace Corps to build houses and bridges in places below the equator. They let Shrimp live with Wallace so Shrimp can go to arts school. Sid and Nancy had no problem shipping me off to a school that was basically a prep academy for Alcoholics Anonymous but they would freak if I asked to move out at sixteen years old.

Lately I have spent the night at Shrimp's a few times. The first time I did, I snuck back home at around six in the morning and went in through the backdoor. I was sure Sid and Nancy would have called out the cops for me by that time. I don't know which I feared worse, that they would send me to some kind of GI Jane school as punishment, or that they would not care.

Leila, the housekeeper, was already up and about, pressing my half-sibs' school uniforms. Leila shook her head at me. "Naughty girl," she said, but I knew she wouldn't rat me out. My parents tweak her nerves as much as mine. My mom is always like "Leila this," "Leila that," "Thank you so much, Leila." It is such a phony act and Nancy only does it when Sid is around. When he's not, she'll be all, "I told you to fold the dinner napkins in a flower shape. Do I have to do *everything*, Leila?"

Nancy is actually super scared of Leila, so every time she says something mean, then she'll air kiss Leila and give Leila the afternoon off. Then Nancy will complain about how no one helps her. Nancy thinks Leila is some kind of superior maid creature because Leila speaks French. Nancy speaks French, *pas.* Nancy likes to act all hyper-chic Society Wife, but if you listen carefully, you can still hear the traces of a Minnesouda cornfield accent, eh?

Nancy is so clueless about the staff's actual lives, I don't think she even knows that Fernando the driver's little grandson had leukemia but bless *Dios* now he's in remission, or that Leila is actually French-Canadian, not French-French. I would like to know if that discrepancy disqualifies Leila from wearing an actual French maid's uniform. When Nancy is not around, Leila and I make lasagna and cookies for Fernando's family.

"Your mother will be up in five minutes," Leila said. She was brewing Nancy's chai tea. "I suggest you go mess up that bed of yours and make it look slept in."

"They didn't notice?" I said.

"*Non,*" Leila said. She could not look me in the eyes.

Five

I'm down with the 411 on my real dad. I read about him in *Who's Who of Corporate America*, in the library at my old school. His name is Frank. He is the boss of a big New York advertising firm. Nancy met Frank when she was a model. That's how she made a living when she lived in New York. She never got very far with her true dream of being a professional dancer.

Frank real-dad has a daughter, Rhonda, and a son, Daniel. Rhonda is such a bad-girl name. She is about fifteen years older than me. I bet when she was in high school she smoked hash in the bathroom and skipped school to hang out in Greenwich Village. She probably wore thick liquid black eyeliner, green lipstick, and black tights with tear holes pinned together with safety pins, just to piss off Frank. If I were named Rhonda, that's what I would do.

That would be so cool to call her up one day and just be like, "Yo Rhonda, this is your flave-flave half-sis Cyd Charisse. Let's hang together but utterly." She would want to brush my hair until it shimmered and then plait it into a dozen braids. She would give me advice about birth control and maybe sometimes, if we were feeling really giggly, she would pass on secret sexual techniques she learned from reading smutty books when she was my age.

Daniel is ten years older than me. If he knew me, he would be really protective of me and call me "kid" all the time. He would muss my hair up, slap me on the back, and always pick me first on his touch football team at Thanksgiving. He would give his friends the old "nuh-uh" when they checked me out. Daniel would have beat the crap out of Justin for getting me into trouble. He would have let me cry on his shoulder after I came back from the clinic, and he would have brought me Dunkin' Donuts in my room afterward and promised never to tell.

Six

Shrimp, Sugar Pie, and I have decided to take Gingerbread on a field trip. Java the Hut has to work, of course, so he let us take his cool new VW beetle. Java's beetle is shiny red with black leather interior. It looks just like a ladybug.

We are going to Santa Cruz. Shrimp is going to surf and Sugar Pie and I are going to take Gingerbread for a walk on the boardwalk.

Nancy threw a freaknik when I said I was spending Sunday with Shrimp and Sugar.

"But that's our family day," she whined. "Dad promised to turn his cell phone off and not go into the office at all. We were going to take you and the kids to the museums in the park and then out for ice cream."

"Oh, could we *really?*" I said, doing my best impression of a Von Trapp child.

I almost felt bad because Nancy's icy white face did look very crushed. Then she snapped, "I don't remember you asking permission to spend the day with *that boy.*" She refuses to call *that boy* "Shrimp." I told her *that boy* also answers to his middle name, Flash. She's sticking with *that boy*.

"I asked you last week right before you had tea with the other ballet moms!" I actually never did ask. I thought about it when she was entertaining my little sister's friends' moms, but I didn't. But since Nancy is famous for not paying attention to me when she is showing off the house to her high-falutin' society friends, I knew I could get away with the lie.

"Well, fine Cyd Charisse, that's just fine, just go. I had to rearrange everyone's schedules so we could spend one day together as a family, but you just go ahead out with *that boy*," Nancy huffed. I could see Leila in the corner of my eye arranging some flowers. Leila was shaking her head that Nancy was letting me off the hook.

When I was leaving, Nancy stopped me at the tall glass door. Her eye makeup looked like it had run from crying, which for Nancy is unusual. She always looks impeccably blonde and perfect.

"How come you hate me?" she said.

That question stopped my heart cold.

"How come *you* hate *me?*" I answered.

I stormed out of the house because I felt I was supposed to after a comment like that, but actually I was very quiet and sad the whole drive down to Santa Cruz. Not even sharing a booty of chocolate with Sugar Pie made me feel better.

"You are a very spoiled child, Miss Sulk," Sugar Pie called to me from the back of the bug when we were about halfway to Santa Cruz. She passed me a miniature Butterfinger bar to show me she meant the comment in a nice way. Sugar and I both love to eat our candy in miniature size, except for Nestlé Crunches, which we both agree are too whamma lamma ding dong to be eaten in miniature. We prefer our Nestlé Crunches to be king-sized.

"Am not!" I said. I did not eat the mini-Butterfinger. Being called spoiled tripped me from a sad mood into a really bad mood. I like to think of myself as misunderstood.

Shrimp laughed as he munched on his frosted straw-berry Pop Tart. "Cyd Charisse, you are too," he said. "I don't know how I ended up with the most spoiled girl in the world. Sugar, it's your fault!" He was teasing and all sing-song. But he must have felt my heart go tumble, because then he leaned over to kiss my cheek, which was not a good idea seeing as how we were driving on a windy road on a cliff over the ocean and Shrimp's hands were jumpy from his morning double espressos. The car swerved suddenly and Shrimp snapped back to attention less than a second before it was too late, right before we went splash over the cliff.

At my commune, there will be no cars. We will probably be so enlightened and unspoiled that we will be able to fly.

"Watch where you're going," I said. I think pouting is stupid but sometimes it serves its purpose. I did not kiss him back since he'd practically just killed us all.

"Burr-ito," Shrimp said. He always says that when I fall into what he calls my "chill factor," all moody and cold.

Sugar was dizzy from the sudden swerve. Maybe it had made her think of her dead Honey's honeymoon. We stopped the car at a rest area because she thought she might need to hurl, but actually she was fine once the car was no longer in motion. Once her hurl urge had passed, Sugar said could we stay here and rest awhile before getting back on the road. Shrimp said that's why they call it a rest area. He put down the backseat of the bug so Sugar could take a little nap. He covered Sugar up with an old mohair blanket which had been laying on the car floor stuck to a piece of bubble gum, and I put Gingerbread in her arms to keep Sugar safe and warm.

While Sugar napped, Shrimp and I walked down a trail toward the ocean. "What are you so tweaked about?" Shrimp said.

I hate it when this happens, but tears started streaming down my face, totally out of control. I was remembering how after we first moved to San Francisco, while Sid was working, Nancy would get bored and lonely from not knowing anybody. Some days she would keep me home from school and we would drive down the highway along the ocean and she wouldn't even mind if I brought Gingerbread along, even though she hates that doll. One thing about my mom is that she is so beautiful, and as we drove along the windy cliff highway, I would feel so secondhand cool sitting next to her in the convertible. I used to want to dress like her, so before we'd leave she'd place a silk scarf identical to hers on my head and tie it under my chin to protect my hair from the wind, and then she'd hold my chin in her soft, perfumed hands and put lipstick on me, then give me an eskimo kiss on my cheek so she wouldn't ruin her lipstick. She always had a spare pair of rhinestone-studded cat-eye sunglasses to place over my eyes. When we got to Santa Cruz, she would buy me cotton candy and take me on the scary rollercoaster, not the kiddie one, even though I was not old enough. I have always been tall and looked a lot older than I am and besides, I would beg her to let me ride. Nancy would scream all bloody hell at the rollercoaster's sudden turns and heart-pounding dips, as I laughed and laughed. You are fearless, she used to say.

I shrugged at Shrimp's question. Sometimes when there's too much to explain it's easier to say nothing. Shrimp looked confused. I was chilling on him and crying and not explaining. He had that look Wallace gets when one of his girlfriends goes postal: "Women!" Sid gets the same look when Nancy complains about how much time he spends being Big Corporate Boss man, and not enough time with the family. It is some kind of universal guy look, a mixture of annoyance, desire, and wishing they could be watching Sports Center instead of witnessing their woman's freak-out.

If Justin had been standing with me in this scene, he would have bailed so fast I wouldn't have been able to emote word one even if I'd wanted to.

Luckily Shrimp did not do that sensitive boy routine and try to hold me and wipe away my tears. Sometimes tears just have to run their course, and it's nice to have a boyfriend who understands that without being either mean or all smothery. When I was finished, we sat down on some rocks overlooking the ocean. I was glad Gingerbread was curled up with Sugar because the ocean breeze was seriously freeze.

Shrimp said, "Let's play Job for a Day," and I brightened up a little. He was eyeing the sun and the surf below and I knew he was jonesing to get back in the car and finish the drive to Santa Cruz. I appreciated him offering to play my favorite game so Sugar could have a rest and I could mellow out.

Shrimp started. "I would like to be the bellman at Campton Place Hotel who looks like the Beefeater guy for a day." The mental image of Shrimp wearing the bellowing bellman costume with the tights and the queer hat and flagging cabs for tourists made me giggle. The uniform would be bigger than him.

"Short-order cook cuz I would like to know how to make perfect eggs," I offered.

"You think in one day you could master perfect scrambled eggs and sunnyside-up eggs and eggs-benedict eggs?" Shrimp asked.

"Everything eggs," I assured him.

"Toll taker at the Golden Gate Bridge," Shrimp said.

I told him, "You would look so cute in that park service uniform."

A ray of sunlight shone right through the platinum spike in his hair, and he grinned. "Ya think?" he said, and in an instant my burr-ito melted.

I said, "Okay, I would like to be the voicemail message lady. 'You have three new messages.' Except I would use some husky porno voice and be all breathy and excited and whatnot. 'To delete this message, press . . . me, lover.'"

Shrimp laughed at my impression. "You'd be good at that, and how funny would that be, too, since you hate to talk on the phone." He thought awhile and then pronounced, "Traffic helicopter guy. I could be, like," he turned on a deep newscaster voice, "'Westbound traffic on the Bay Bridge is backed up to the Maze, metering lights are turned on, and thanks to Bob of the phone force who called in to report an accident in the far right lane of the Bay Bridge just after the island. Suckers!'"

"Excellent!" I said. "Weather girl. Except I would wear super short skirts with slits on the side and go-go boots and grow my fingernails real long and then paint them black so's they would look like a pointer on the weather map."

"Them's some weather I'd be watching," Shrimp said. "Art director and executive vice president of Pop Tarts."

"Brown-sugar division?" I asked.

"But fer sure."

"That's boss," I said. "I would like to be a See's Candy lady so I could wear that white uniform and make people happy when I give them their free sample."

"Okay," Shrimp said, "just don't give people white chocolate samples. Nobody actually likes white chocolate and it is such a gyp to get that for your free sample."

"You are so right," I said.

One time I tried to play Job for a Day with Justin and the only thing he could think up was quarterback for the New England Patriots. How *clever*.

"Census taker," Shrimp pronounced.

"But people might be really rude to you," I said.

"That's why it's a job for only a day," Shrimp reminded me. "You can do anything for a day."

Childbirth is one job I'm glad to keep off my résumé, even for just a day. Nancy was in labor for a whole day when my little brother was born. She said it was the most painful experience of her whole life and she'd thought since I was an easy birth that labor was always that easy. She made Sid take her to a spa in Arizona a month later and while they were gone Leila let me feed my half-brother his bottle.

Feeding babies is not so bad, actually. They scream and scream so you think your eardrums will burst, but when the bottle hits their mouth, you can feel their whole body relax and like become part of you as the baby nestles in your arms. My little brother used to wrap his little hand around my thumb when I fed him, and then totally coo and flirt with me while he was feeding. He was the cutest thing and I almost was totally in love with him. I guess you could say I was half in love with him because he was my half-brother, but then when Nancy came back she would never let me hold him and Sid always made me wash my hands before I could be near him. Now that baby is in third grade and only likes to play with guns and toys that make exploding sounds. He still loves me best, though.

When I woke up this morning, I looked at the date on my Swiss Army watch and realized today was the day the doctor estimated as my baby's due date. That's when I called Shrimp and asked could we take a field trip. If things were different, I could have been giving birth about now. That baby would have my black hair and Justin's baby blue eyes. Maybe it was a girl and I could have dressed her up in silk scarves, cat-eye sunglasses, and red lipstick and given her eskimo kisses. I cannot picture that baby any more than that.

Seven

Despite what Nancy says, I am not all doom and gloom, you know. I can let loose. I can have fun.

I think.

Once we got to Santa Cruz, Sugar, Gingerbread, and I sunbathed on the beach awhile, catching some rays and listening to the ocean roar while Shrimp surfed. A Mexican mariachi band played a song from a nearby pier that sounded like an accordian lullaby. I stood up and showed Sugar my harem dance, where I lightly gyrate my hips and move my hands and fingers in cool shapes like I saw once in this documentary about dancers from the island of Bali. While I dance I hum this possessed chant like I am in an Islamic mosque even though my dance is probably sacrilegious.

"Do you like my dance?" I asked Sugar.

"I like your dance," Sugar said. "But I'm thinking it's not a good idea for a nice young lady to perform such a dance while wearing a string bikini and see-through wrap skirt on a beach swarming with young men. Could get you into trouble."

Twirling my head round and round, I pulled the hairpins out from the top of my head so my long black hair swished over my back as I harem-danced in time to the beautiful Mexican lullaby. I winked at Gingerbread. She winked back. She loves my harem dance.

"Don't worry about me, Sugar," I said. "I've already been in enough trouble for a lifetime. I might have run out of trouble."

"Girl, you look like trouble."

"Thank you, Sugar," I said.

For a second I had an urge to tell Sugar about last fall, when I was really in trouble. I have not even told Shrimp about that. The only people who know are Justin and my real dad, and that's only because I had no *dinero* to take care of my little *problemo,* and Justin kept promising to get the money and every day that passed I threw up more and more but no money from Justin. One day I was almost out of excuses for getting out of gym class, so while I was in the nurse's office I called Manhattan information when the nurse wasn't in the room and I got the listing for Frank real-dad's company. I called the company switchboard and asked for him but they switched me to his secretary. She had this thick, nasal New York accent. I said, I would like to speak with Frank, please, and she said, Who's calling and I said, Please tell him it's Cyd Charisse. Right, the secretary said, and I'm Greta Garbo. I get that all the time. But maybe she heard the panic in my voice and maybe she was impressed that I used the word "please" twice, because when I asked for him a second time, she put me on hold and sounded surprised when she returned to the line and said he would be right with me.

"What's up, kiddo?" he said when he picked up the phone. His voice was all cheery and familiar, like this wasn't the first time we had talked since that time at the airport when I was five and he bought me Gingerbread. He did not have me on speakerphone like Sid-dad always does and he was a little out of breath, like he had just bolted up from his chair and run to close his executive office door so his un-Greta Garbo secretary would not hear him.

I couldn't believe it was actually him on the phone. I wished I could tape-record his voice so I would never forget the sound of it. "I still have Gingerbread," I told him, speaking softly.

"What's Gingerbread?" he said. He almost sounded annoyed, like he was worried I was speaking in some cryptic code.

What's Gingerbread? I couldn't believe my ears. I felt so betrayed I wanted to scream but instead I got mad and went straight to the point. "I need three hundred dollars," I said, matching his tone of voice. "I'm in trouble."

"What kind of trouble?" he asked.

"What kind do you *think?*" I said. That was all I needed to say. He wired the money to me by dinnertime that night. So counting the time when I was five, that call made it two times I have spoken to my real father in my life.

I stopped my harem dance to admire Shrimp right as his tight little bod grabbed a killer tall wave and the ocean curl rose over his head and the painted skull at the tip of his surfboard peeked through the water. It was like this perfect Shrimp moment. I asked Sugar, "Did you ever have a boyfriend where right away it felt like you just belonged together, like you had known that person your whole life?"

"I did," Sugar said. "'Cept turned out he felt that way about my sister, too."

Ouch.

"Maybe you just haven't found your soulmate yet," I told her. "C'mon, let's go find him." I dragged her off the sand and, arm in arm, we headed for the boardwalk. As we walked along the beach, our toes cushioned in soft, warm sand, I asked Sugar, "Do you really think I'm spoiled?"

"Yes, baby," she said. "You do not even begin to understand the privilege you have had in your life. But your heart is solid gold. That's what's important."

I made a mental note to tell Shrimp I wanted to be a solid gold one-hit wonder pop singer next time we played Job for a Day. And I am also going to make it my mission to find Sugar her King Soulmate.

We ate lunch at a diner and afterward we shared a piece of chocolate pie and then Sugar Pie read the tarot cards for me. First she had me shuffle her ancient deck of cards, and she told me to concentrate on a question, or a certain issue, to which I would like answers or guidance. *Shrimp Shrimp Shrimp,* I thought as I shuffled the deck, and separated the cards into three piles. I was glad the day with my two favorite people was turning out so much more pleasant than spending the day giving birth to a baby.

Sugar placed her hands over my three piles of cards to feel which pile had the most energy rising from it. After choosing the middle pile, she proceeded to lay down three cards when suddenly her head popped up and her eyes flashed at me.

"Seems like you got yourself into some deep trouble, Cyd Charisse," she said. Her eyes softened as she continued laying out the cards. It was like I could feel her heart reaching out to me in concern. When she finished laying down the cards, she squeezed my hand and said, "Little girl, is there anything you want to tell me about?"

I smiled because it's not often that a girl as tall as me gets called "little," and it's not often that I smile. My dad Sid is the only other person who calls me "little girl." The nickname is our little joke. I am three inches taller than him.

When I didn't answer her question, Sugar said, "Well, what was on your mind when you shuffled the cards?"

I said, "I want to know about my future with Shrimp and whether I will grow another bra size."

She laughed and then said, "That's all?"

Sometimes the need to let go of a secret can be overwhelming. I said, "Maybe if things had been different I might have been doing something very different today other than coming to Santa Cruz with you and Shrimp." Feeling like if just one person I cared about knew, then maybe it wouldn't hurt so much. I whispered, "Like having a baby."

Sugar pointed at the Seven and Five of Swords cards and nodded her head, like she was doing the math from the cards and what I had just told her. "Of course," she whispered. "Betrayal." She was not all weepy and oh-let-me-hold-you-poor-baby. She knew what was on my mind. "You did the right thing," she said, and a massive tide of relief swept through me. "See that Five of Cups card?" she asked. "Notice how two cups are still standing upright? What you can learn from those cards is, maybe you've been hurt, but not all is lost."

Little tiny tears formed in my eyes but I kept them back. "I didn't want to hurt it," I said, refusing to choke on the almost-tears. "I just wasn't ready."

"You did the right thing, Cyd Charisse," Sugar Pie repeated. She laid down another card and pointed to the card with the knives staking through a heart. "I can see you didn't get much help from that sorry thing you used to call 'boyfriend.'"

I shook my head. I didn't want to go there. It's funny to think that a year ago I was so totally obsessed with Justin, and now I am grateful to be on the opposite end of the country from him. He still tries to call me. I asked Leila to please stop giving me his phone messages.

Sugar said, "Cyd Charisse, I have never told anyone about this before, but remember that story I told you about my sister Honey running off with my man?"

I nodded.

"Well, the part of that story I leave out is that the same day I found out they were dead, I found out I was pregnant. Sounds like something out a soap opera, I know, but life is funny, baby, and that's no joke." She nodded solemnly.

"What did you do?"

"I was eighteen years old, unmarried, no job, just lost my Honey and my honey. I did what you did. Only it wasn't legal then and it was in a back alley basement of the colored doctor. Most painful experience of my life." Sugar's beautiful café-au-lait-colored skin paled at the memory. I remembered the horrible cramping in my stomach after the procedure, which was performed in a safe and legal environment, so I could only imagine what Sugar must have experienced fifty years ago.

"Are you ever sorry you did?" I asked. Because that's what haunts me, that later on, I will want to, and not be able to.

"Never," Sugar said. I believed her, kinda. "If I hadn't done it, I never would have made my way to California. Got to New York, Paris, Chicago, all them places before coming here. Had me some adventures." Her coral lips had come back to color and she smiled. "You know, there was a time I thought the world was over for me. And I was but eighteen years old. Thought I had no life left to live. And I look at these cards in front of me, and I see that's how you've been feeling. But the times in your life—good and bad, and they'll be lots of both—are still ahead of you. Now's the time for you to think about your future, making new friends, seeing new places. You might have been to hell and back, girl, but losing yourself in Shrimp and spending the rest of your time with this old lady is not all that's in the cards for you."

Sugar laid down a new card. "The future," she said. "See the Fool there? He's innocent, fearless, about to go off the edge of a cliff. That card can tell you that you just don't know what's around the corner. Looks to me like some new people are coming into your life, and some old ones coming back in. Like you're going back to new-old places."

"Huh?" I said. "Not boarding school!"

"Maybe not boarding school. But definitely back to an old place. Here's the Chariot card. Things change quickly, sometimes even backward."

Bor-ing. I asked Sugar, "Is Shrimp my soulmate? How come there's no Lovers card here?"

"Maybe you're going to have many soulmates in your life," Sugar said. "Which would be the opposite of me. I had many loves but only one soulmate. Maybe you'll have many soulmates but only one true love. You did get the Ten of Pentacles card. That card can indicate someone you got a real soul connection with."

"Shrimp!" I said.

Sugar laughed. "Who said I was talking about Shrimp?"

Eight

"Do you think Sugar was trying to mess with my mind?" I asked Shrimp later that night after we'd dropped Sugar back at the home.

We were making out in the back seat of the bug, parked under dripping trees on a hill at Lands End which overlooks the Pacific Ocean and the Golden Gate Bridge. Shrimp sighed. This was about the sixth time I had asked him.

He wriggled his hand out from under my shirt, sat up, and cinched the strings on his drawstring shorts, then leaned down to caress my cheek. "No, Cyd," he said, "I don't think Sugar was trying to mess with your mind. I think she was trying to tell you to make more friends besides me and her, and to be open to the possibility that we might not be together for all time."

He said it so casually. I hoped Gingerbread had covered her ears. "You don't think we'll be together for all time?" I said. My voice was hurried and anxious, shocked. The thought of!

The night was pitch black except for the stars twinkling through the VW bug's sunroof, but I could see his pupils dilating in fear of having to decide this huge thing right now. "I don't know," he said. "I never really thought about it. I dig you mucho. But I barely know what I'm going to paint tomorrow, or where I'll want to surf next weekend, much less who I'm going to be with for eternity. What do you think, that we'll be together for all time?"

"Now I don't," I said, and shoved his body off of mine. I was getting really aggravated. I adore Shrimp and maybe one day when I'm thirty or something I will want to marry him if I ever decide I believe in marriage, but that's forever away and right now it's not like I need to spend every waking second with him. I guess I just wanted to know that when he pictured his future, I was in it. And since he wouldn't make that proclamation, I announced, "Maybe the tarot cards were right. Maybe you're not my soulmate."

Shrimp sighed again. "Or maybe you're making the tarot cards be right."

"You don't believe in the tarot, do you?" I said.

He did not even hesitate. "Nope," he said.

"So you think Sugar is a liar?" I asked.

"I didn't say that," he said. He took a deep breath, signaling he was about to spout more than his usual minimal sentence comments. "I said I don't believe in those cards any more than I believe that fate is predetermined and we have no choice about it. I'm saying that if you decide that the tarot card says I am not your soulmate or your eternal whatever, then maybe now you're about to make it a self-fulfilling prophecy."

"Mister Big Words!" I accused, then wished I had some automatic smacking device I could use on myself. I had just pulled a Nancy, who always gives Sid or me stupid names when we have said something totally smart and she can't think of anything smart to say back quickly. Which is how Sid often gets called "Mister All-Important Executive Man," and I become "Miss Sullen Teen Nightmare."

"'Mister Big Words,'" Shrimp repeated, laughing, like I had just broken through to a whole new undiscovered level of uncool. "Cyd Charisse, you are just delicious."

He leaned down to kiss me but I was giggling, too. Fight forgotten. I reached my arms out to him and he snuggled in. We didn't do It. Just looked at the moon and stars through the sunroof as Shrimp whispered a rap song in my ear. *Mister Big Words. Lover of interdimensional planetary combustolary wordiness bo-bo-birdiness. Cyd Charisse and Shrimp in the Land of Big Words, flying through multisyllabic iambic pentameter haiku why you juvenile court detention retention. Word.*

When he finished, I whispered back in his ear, "I love you."

"Yeah," he mumbled in that sexy deep voice, "ditto."

For a little guy, he sure could keep a girl warm.

Nine

After Shrimp dropped me off at home, I went in through the back door. Sid and Nancy were talking in his study, drinking martinis. They must have had a really tiring day because normally Sid drinks only the martinis I make for him. When I was younger, Sid used to pay me a dollar to make his martinis and pack the tip of his cigar before he had his evening smoke. Sid says I am his perfect creation, that only I make the perfect martini.

Nancy was saying to Sid, "Well, at least she's not dating a drug dealer or turning up pregnant. I guess we should be grateful for that."

I came this close to letting out a gigantic "HAH!" from the other side of the sliding mahogany study door.

"Nancy," Sid said. A warm feeling of comfort and safety came over me, which I realized was caused by the smell of Sid's cigar. "Relax. I think the recovering little hellion's bad times are behind her. Frankly, I don't see why you're so concerned about *that boy*. Seems like since they've been together, she's managed not to be arrested for shoplifting or get kicked out of school. He's a good enough kid. Did you know he's going to work part-time at the Java the Hut store at Ocean Beach? Good thing for a young person, holding a job."

"She spends all her time with him!" Nancy shrieked. "We don't know anything about his family! At least that Justin boy, we knew of his family."

"If you ask me, Justin was Cyd Charisse's trouble, not this Shrimp fellow." The dirty little secret in our family is that Sid-dad loves all his children, but I am his pet. He always defends me to Nancy. Drives her nuts.

"How do you know so much about *that boy,* Mister Sudden Empathy?"

"Maybe if you spent some time actually talking to him instead of scowling at his hair or his clothes or his way of mumbling, you'd get to know him, too. Kids are like dogs, Nancy. They know who their friends are."

"But . . ." Nancy groaned.

"Enough!" Sid said. This Cyd silently thanked him and went upstairs to her room. Wowsa, he had really stood up for Shrimp. I know for a fact that Sid shudders in horror every time he witnesses Shrimp's spiked platinum hair and sharktooth necklace. Probably Sid just wanted to be contrary to Nancy. That's how they get along.

When I got to my room, I flopped on my puke princess bed. A voice called out "Ouch!" I rolled over onto my stomach and skooched to the end of the bed to see what creature lay underneath.

"That bounce hit my head!" my nine-year-old brother said.

"So maybe some little pest shouldn't hide under there," I said.

Josh crawled out from underneath my bed and did this bizarre lickety-split marathon run around my room, banging his fist into each corner as he passed it, like he was marking territory. This is not a boy who worries about my parents catching him awake after bedtime.

"Come here, Hyper Boy," I said. I turned down my bedsheets to make room for him. He did a divebomb into my bed as I pulled the next Narnia book out from my nightstand.

"Do the voices! Do the voices!" he cried out. He is a sucker for my Aslan.

"Okay," I said, "but you have to be quiet."

Josh smacked his hands over his lips, producing loud blubbering noises. I closed the book and started to put it away.

"Okay okay okay okay okay okay okay," Josh rush-whispered. "I'll be extra super-duper quiet." He banged his head against my shoulder a few times before nestling it inside my hip. I flicked his head just for fun and then started to read.

I am the only person for whom he will be quiet and calm at night. He drives Leila nuts and I think he is responsible for all the new gray hairs on Nancy's head that she has to have colored out, despite Nancy's claim that I am the root of her gray hair woes.

"I like it when you put me to bed, Cyd Charisse," Josh whispered. I knew it took superhuman willpower for him not to shout. "I like it better when you are here instead of away at school."

"Well, don't get too used to me," I said. "I haven't decided for sure that I am staying."

Ten

I am thinking of moving my commune to Siberia. We will invite Wallace and his new girlfriend, Delia. She is from Alaska and probably knows everything about wild cold wilderness situations. Wallace and Delia could figure out how to make iced coffee igloos for us to live in. We'll call them "coffeegloos." Everybody might have a hard time sleeping because the coffeegloos' walls give off a caffeine-laced aura, so we could tell ghost stories. We'd listen to the wind whir and the coyotes howl and wear those cool fur hats with the flaps on the ears. Probably Wallace and Shrimp will have to learn to ice fish even though they're vegetarians. Survival is key. They will sit at the hole in the ice for hours and hours, not talking but most likely communicating telepathically. Delia and I will dance around the coffeegloos while they are gone and listen to our voices echo at the crests of the plains. I'm fairly sure no one else I know will want to visit my commune in Siberia, but that will give us a chance to get to know the natives better. They will teach us how to make borscht and tell us about the olden days, when Siberia housed Stalin's prison camps. We won't be scared.

Eleven

I have figured out a brilliant plan to drive Nancy crazy. I have a summer job at Java the Hut. Nancy can't say anything about it because Sid thinks young people should have jobs, like he did when he was a kid and had to walk five miles to school in the snow every morning before he became a self-made gazillionaire. Sid thinks having a summer job will "straighten the little hellion out," even if it is working with *that boy*.

Plus now I can thank Shrimp and Sugar not to call Cyd Charisse "spoiled" any more, thankyouverymuch.

I guess I am lucky because I don't need to work for money. Actually, I don't really care about whether or not I have money. Sugar says that is a rich person's conceit, but I told her it's not my fault Sid is rich and Sugar agreed, that's true. Anyway, I am not a mall junkie kind of girl who needs to save money for hair clips and glitter makeup and boy band CDs. Excuse me while I go retch at that thought.

So I try not to use the fact that I don't actually need the Java the Hut job as a reason to be rude to customers who complain that their coffee is not hot enough or who say "I asked for a cappuccino and you gave me a latte," huff, when I know for certain the word *latte* was uttered to me. I also try not to roll my eyes at customers who assume that because I am a teenager working for minimum wage and what barely counts as tips that they need to speak extra slowly to me. "Miss, could . . . I . . . please . . . have . . . a . . . single . . .

blended . . . decaf . . . capp . . . with . . . extra . . . foam? Did you get that? Are you sure? Want to repeat it back to me?"

If you have to have a job, Java the Hut is the place to be. Maybe because the coffeehouse is located all the way out in foggy and cold Ocean Beach, but everyone is pretty mellow. The place has old bean bags for chairs and sofas from the Salvation Army and ancient books on bookshelves which customers actually read and there is always the smell of saltwater mixing in with the coffee scent. Wallace has even installed a special rack for customers to park their surfboards. What is extra cool is that since the surf at Ocean Beach is so fierce, the surfers have to be extra strong to swim out. Which means Cyd Charisse gets to admire some customers with buff bods and tight pecs in wet suits all day long, uh-huh.

Some establishments have signs saying "Shirt and shoes required." At Java the Hut, shirts and shoes are optional if you don't mind freezing in the Ocean Beach chill, but you can check your perkiness at the door. I mean, this is not a place where employees have to ask would you like to super size that order and then offer a pearly smile.

Delia, who is the daytime assistant manager and Java's girlfriend, makes the days go by quickly. She is a dancer studying at San Francisco State. She stands on her toes when she is grinding coffee and grooves to a hip-hop beat as she clears tables. She always has funky music blaring at the store. She likes to shake her booty as she adds register receipts at the end of the day, singing, "Make my funk the P-Funk, I wants to get funked up."

Delia says how can I have a name like Cyd Charisse and not want to be a dancer. Have you ever actually watched a movie where Cyd Charisse danced? she asked. Not really, I said. Delia is trying to get me to come to the modern dance class she teaches at a nearby dance studio, but when I picture myself there, I see myself wearing a tiara and a tulle tutu, standing on tippy toes in combat boots and frowning. No thank you.

Nancy has figured out a way to get back at me for having a summer job. She sends Fernando, the driver, over to Ocean Beach in the Mercedes with the dark tinted windows to pick me up after my shift. I have offered Fernando my whole salary as hush money to not come pick me up, but he won't take it. "Orders is orders," he said, which I understand. I know the difference between a latte and a cappuccino.

Fernando drinks straight black coffee every day while he waits for me to finish washing dishes and sweeping the kitchen. That's how I figured out something about Fernando. He is Sugar's soulmate. Every day after I give Fernando his black coffee, I clock his sugar-pouring time and it's about ten whole seconds. That's a lot of sugar for a guy with a long red scar on his face, the kind of leather face you would never think to ask, "Can I make you an espresso drink this evening?" I mean, he is black coffee and then some. Some sugar.

Fernando is not that old, even though he is a grandpa. He is a widower. I would say he is in his early sixties, which is young for Sugar, but so what. A good man is a good man, no matter what age. He got the long red scar going down the side of his face during the civil war in Nicaragua. That's all he'll tell me about it. Fernando is not exactly a talkative kind of guy, so I don't know much about him. I do know for a fact that he was not named for the ABBA song "Fernando."

I like Fernando and I am totally going to hook him up with Sugar but I'm sorry to say I am going to have to ditch him, orders or no orders. Twilight after work is Shrimp and Wallace's sacred surf time, and Delia and I would like to start sunset barbecuing so we can all eat dinner together when the moonlight strikes. See, I am so ready for a commune situation. Have grill, will commune.

In exchange for being allowed to have a job, I have promised to be a model citizen daughter, and for these first few weeks working at Java the Hut, I have been. I have let Fernando pick me up at work and I have eaten dinner with the fam every night. My shoplifting days are over, I actually got decent grades last term, and I have not made a razor design on any part of my body in eons. I have confined my Shrimp time to making out with him in the Java the Hut supply closet and quick feels on the cold hard sand at the beach during our breaks, but enough is enough. A girl can only be dutiful for so long. The summer solstice is only days away, and Delia and I are planning a party at Wallace and Shrimp's house and I am spending the night whether Sid and Nancy notice or not. I will be as wild as I wanna be.

Twelve

Shrimp is totally my main ingredient, but can I just confess that I would not mind a little side order of Java sometime? Shrimp's brother is hot hot hot. Wallace is a little taller than Shrimp, but way more filled out in his wet suit. Wallace has some serious drool-worthy upper body happening and beautiful long dirty blond hair which he wears pulled back in a ponytail, but not in a gay way like Fabio. And he has smoldering gray eyes that burn when Java the Hut receipts don't add up, or when delivery people are late, or when he's been working since five in the morning and goes out surfing at the end of the day and the waves are lame and the sun is bright instead of obscured by broody fog which means that tourists are everywhere.

I suppose I will burn in hell like in some Greek tragedy for lusting after my boyfriend's brother, he who also happens to be the boyfriend of my new friend Delia from Alaska. But I also suppose there is a long list of deeds for which I might burn in hell, so why not add secret crush on my boyfriend's brother.

Anyway, it is not the dangerous type of crush where I will play all Lolita and entice Wallace into some skanky love triangle. Spare me. Wallace is just like this aesthetic dream that if I were an artist I would paint and be tortured by and long for always, but never have.

It's hard not to sigh at those brothers while staring at them through binoculars from the roof deck of Wallace and Shrimp's house. Those boys are sumpin' sumpin'. The sun was just falling over the ocean horizon as Shrimp and Wallace, wet-suited and carrying their boards under their arms, crossed over Great Highway back toward the house. Their heads were hunched over at the same exact angle and the wind was whipping their wet hair so they looked almost like identical surf punks.

Nine o'clock in the evening on the longest day of the year, and Delia and I were summer-solstice barbecuing on a deck built on the roof of Shrimp and Wallace's house as we watched the sun set over the Pacific. We were making scrumptious veggieburgers din-dins for our menfolk to eat once they jumped out of the surf.

Curiosity was burning through my skin and I wanted to ask Delia, What is it like to touch Wallace? To feel the weight of him on you? Luckily before I spoke, my mind went ding-ding-ding-danger, and instead I said to Delia, "How come you came to San Francisco from Alaska?" I suppose I don't really care how or why Delia came to be here, I just think it is cool to be from some remote wilderness with a cool name like *A-la-ska,* and anyway it is fun listening to Delia talk because she has this husky deep voice which totally does not match the way she looks, little miss slip dresses and ballet pliés and jettés as she walks.

"I ran out of dance teachers in Alaska," Delia said. "And who doesn't want to live in San Francisco?"

I don't want to live in San Francisco. I don't mind living here because it is insanely beautiful, but I will bail for my commune or to move to New York and wear all black at the first opportunity.

"Did you live in an igloo in Alaska?" I asked.

Delia laughed like I am uproarious. "Hardly, Cyd

Charisse," she said. "I grew up in a nice suburban house in Anchorage with running water and cable TV. Winters were cold and summers gorgeous and dancing, always."

"Oh," I said. I must admit that I was disappointed.

I was not disappointed that I managed to ditch Fernando. I told him to pick me up at Sugar's nursing home after work, knowing that by the time Fernando figured out that I was not at Sugar's, Java the Hut would be closed and we would be barbecuing veggieburgers and Fernando would be in love with Sugar. Done deal.

By the ringing of the phone as I stared at Shrimp and Wallace through the binoculars, I knew it was safe to say that Fernando had caught on.

"*Hola,*" I said into the cordless.

"Very funny," Fernando said back.

"Do you totally love Sugar?" I asked.

Fernando pretended he didn't hear my question. "You want to tell your mother about this, or should I?"

I wasn't sure. I had assumed Fernando would tell her, if she was even paying attention. No biggity.

Sugar got on the line and said, "Cyd Charisse, you bad girl. Are you trying to get Fernando in trouble?"

"Fernando won't be in trouble, Sugs. I will."

Sugar's sigh was a mile long. "No, baby. It is Fernando's responsibility to see that you come home from work every evening. That was the agreement with your parents. He doesn't come home with you, he's in trouble."

"But that's so unfair!" I said.

"Exactly," Sugar said, and handed the phone back to Fernando.

"*Chiquita bonita?*" he asked.

"I'll call Nancy now," I said. "I'll tell her I bailed on you."

"Adios," Fernando said. Click-ito.

Here's how I know I have entered a total freak zone. When I called Nancy, she said fine that I had dinner at Shrimp's, just to not come home too late. She was hostessing a grand soirée for her society friends, so I'm guessing she was relieved not to have me traipsing through the door and her having to explain to all those biddies about why her daughter has . . . gasp . . . a J-O-B . . . gasp . . . in Ocean Beach! Ocean Where? they would have asked, like the Ocean Beach neighborhood isn't four miles from their Pacific Heights mansions.

"I'm free!" I sang out as Shrimp walked through the deck and hugged me from behind. I did not care that his wet suit was still damp or that his head nuzzled inside my neck was dripping chill water down my chest. He felt just right.

La vie en Cyd Charisse is getting awfully cozy, I thought. I have not been in trouble in ages, I have a totally boss boyfriend, a responsible summer job, and Nancy is even doling out permission slips for hanging out with *that boy*. I might be getting bored, I realized, as I turned around to plant one on Shrimp, but over my shoulder I checked out Wallace and noticed that he was totally checking me out too.

Danger.

Thirteen

"You're cool," Wallace mumbled to me in the moonlight. Delia and Shrimp were passed out in their sleeping bags on either side of us. Only the sound of the crashing waves drowned out their snores.

How could I sleep when Java the Hut with the peppermint-tea breath was telling me stories all night, with his dreamy long hair hanging down over his shoulders and his smoldering eyes burning through my moonlit gaze. Oh lordy, pray for me now, Sugar Pie would have said if she were here now.

"Yup," I said back to Wallace, and then thought, *Yup?* Cyd Charisse, thy vocab is doth lacking.

I must be some kind of a gravedigger because Wallace is almost a quarter of a century old and I totally want to unzip that sleeping bag of his and squeeze on in.

On my commune, it will be okay to love two brothers, just not at the same time.

After Shrimp and Delia fell asleep, Wallace and I started talking about past loves. I told him about my first boyfriend, Luke, when I was fourteen but almost fifteen. Luke was seventeen and rode a motorcycle. Actually, it was a moped and he sucked at riding it. He was always wiping out in the parking lot. No wonder he had to be a Latin tutor, there had to be something for him to be good at.

One other thing Luke was good at was kissing. When we were supposed to be studying declensions, he was actually teaching me how to kiss using all the parts in my mouth—

my lips, my tongue, my teeth—and how to kiss with Hershey's chocolate syrup on my tongue and marshmallow fluff on his. Disgusting—maybe, but yummy—definitely. Sometimes we kissed shotgun style using a Coke can cradling Jamaican weed. I got bored with the weed thing a long time ago, but the soul kissing thing is a keeper.

No matter how many varieties of substances Luke abused, or how many leather jackets he wore or how long his hair got or how much he tried to look like Kurt Cobain, he could not pull off the whole Angry Young Man thing. The boy was a bottom-line brainiac who was destined to go to Harvard and be a neuro-chem-atomic-physics genius, regardless of the fact that he had perfected the art of Frenching, and it is my hope that one day when he wins the Nobel Prize, he will remember it was me who told him that he was so totally just a geek who could make out like a champion but really, ditch the rebel routine and get back to the books.

Luke dumped me for a mathlete girl who put out. But by that time Justin's bulky biceps and lacrosse calves had entered into my line of hormonally challenged vision, and I was like, Luke who? and I gave it up to Justin in a heartbeat. *Quid pro quo.* I mean Justin just had the body of a god. Forgive me, but it's true. I just wanted to run my hands all over him, all the time. That's how trouble starts, see.

How come on TV shows where teens are having sex it's always such a naughty thing, or something that has to be talked about over and over until the characters can finally get it on. In real life, it is not so hard. Look, want, touch, trouble.

Sex doesn't always end in trouble. On TV, if you are a teen and you are having sex, you are either (a) not a major character or (b) going to have to learn an Important Lesson, whether it's pregnancy, AIDS, or any other form of sexually transmitted disease, or you are going to suffer through *mucho* parental freak-out scenes.

Most people I know my age who are doing it just do it, they don't talk about it forever and ever, and they certainly don't tolerate talking about it with their parents. Not everyone has to have a little morality lesson like I did. Because the truth is, you never see those teens who talk and talk and talk about sex on TV ever really going after each other all hot and heavy. Because what is supposed to be a secret is that—shh, say it quiet—sex can be quite nice, thankyouverymuch. But it's better when it's with a person you care about as much as you want to grope.

Wallace's first love was an Australian-Indonesian girl named Lucinda. Lucinda had azure eyes the color of the tropical sea and long blue-black hair falling to her waist. He met her the year he spent backpacking across Asia before going to college. Lucinda's skin was a bright orange-brown sunset and she was always saying "gerr-ate!" for "great!" in this Australian accent like her Australian father. Lucinda wore silk sarong skirts and Wallace dressed in grass tiki-things and together they liked to sneak off and make love under waterfalls and wrap tight around each other in the warm Indian Ocean, I'm fairly sure.

Lucinda's family lived in a hut on the beach. Her dad was a coffee exporter. That's how Java the Hut was born, learning the trade from Lucinda's pops. Dig?

I asked Wallace how come you didn't stay in Indonesia and marry Lucinda and have Californian-American Australian-Indonesian babies? Because you could tell by the way he talked about Lucinda that she was the love of his life. Wallace answered, I wanted to backpack in Nepal and India and Vietnam, and Lucinda didn't want to go so far away from her parents. I still wanted to go to college. So I left. I was young and I was stupid.

Oh, I said. Right.

I wonder if Lucinda pines for Wallace under the Balinese moon now the way I do under the Ocean Beach, San Francisco, moon. I wonder if we met if she wouldn't mind teaching me how to do that funky Indonesian dance with the curly hands and sexy-swish hips. I wonder if a dingo would eat her baby if she had one. Maybe she had Wallace's secret love child and a dingo ate it one time when she was visiting her grandparents in Australia and now she is like totally traumatized and never leaves her hut even though her mom is always trying to make her dance and be happy again.

I wonder if Lucinda has forgotten Wallace after almost six years.

Doubt it.

I told Wallace, "That is so cool how your parents let Shrimp live with you while they are digging ditches and whatnot."

Wallace laughed but his eyes were not smiling. "It's not so cool," he mumbled.

"*Que?*" I asked. No way having no parents around could be anything less than *splendido*.

Wallace adopted an adult tone which sounded totally queer. He said, "The kid needs his parents, that's all. He's still a kid, and a kid's parents should be with him, not making selfish attempts to recapture their youths by thinking they're helping people who don't need them nearly as much as their son does. I love having him around, don't get me wrong, it's just that . . . I'm not his parents, y'know?"

It was funny to hear Shrimp called "kid." Call me innocent, but I tend not to think of the guy I am fooling around with as "kid." "Kid" to me is a shorty squirt like my little Hyper Boy brother Josh, who likes to make burping noises and open his mouth wide when he's eating so you can see he is eating rocky road ice cream with yellow and red Gummy Bears. "Kid" to me is not the King of Hearts who likes to slow dance against me in his wet suit even when there is no music playing.

"No, I don't know," I told Wallace. Parents who leave their teenager alone to grow up in peace would have to be the coolest.

I guess.

If I could ditch my 'rents, I would stay on this rooftop in a sleeping bag sandwiched between the two cutest brothers in the world forever and ever. Who knew life could be this good?

Of course, Nancy's tentacles must have radared my pleasure back to her nightmares, because all of a sudden we heard a very loud HONK coming from the street. The kind of HONK that can only come at one in the morning from my stepfather's armored Mercedes, with a large, scarred, black-coffee-drinking Fernando at the wheel.

"Bugger!" I said. I was up and out of the sleeping bag before Wallace could explain about why their parents should not be halfway around the world.

Shrimp had woken up from the sound of the HONK. He knew the score.

"Bye, babe," he murmured as I raced toward the stair-way leading downstairs. His outstretched hand brushed the ankle bracelet he'd made me as I stormed past him.

He is a BABE BABE BABE and so is his brother and I am not going to tolerate this interference from my parental units any longer.

Fourteen

When I got home I found that a little slumber party had been going on in Pacific Heights as well. The kind of slumber party that happens when Nancy wakes up in the middle of the night and comes into my room to see if I am sleeping or if I am awake and picking the cuticles on my fingers or some other kind of mental behavior, but instead Nancy finds me gone, and proceeds to wake the whole house up with her screeching and shrieking.

My little sister Ashley was waiting for me at the door when Fernando and I drove up.

"Cyd Charisse's Pieces is home and she's in fucking trou-trou-trouble!" she singsonged. She is six going on sixteen and may be more of a terror than Hyper Boy Josh. She is an angel-faced, gutter-mouthed little pudge. I think she is adorable. You will never catch me telling her that.

I didn't used to think Ash was adorable because she was always going through my stuff, but then Nancy had my room redecorated and now I no longer have any desire to keep my stuff in that puke princess room. Besides, I am not the type of girl to keep a diary with a lock and key. I keep all my secrets in my head, where no one besides myself and Gingerbread, who is a telepath, can mess around. All my other important stuff—old letters from Justin, drawings by Shrimp, my birth control prescription, the "Home Sweet Home" pillow I embroidered for Gingerbread in home ec class—I keep in a box in Sugar Pie's room at the home. She never goes through my stuff. She is too busy making money playing cards and reading old folks' tarots.

Ash was spilling out of the fairy costume that she will go schiz if you try to make her take off. She stood in the driveway waving her rhinestone fairy wand at me, dressed in pink tights, pink leotard, pink tulle skirt, with a rhinestone tiara on her head and a pink Kool-Aid moustache over her mouth.

I poked her pudge stomach as I breezed by her. "Don't touch my baby fat!" she called after me.

If I actually considered myself to be part of this family, I would say we are a family of complete freaks.

"It's not baby fat," I said back. "It's those Twinkies you keep hidden under your bed that no one besides you and the rats who crawl under your bed know about."

Don't tell me who's in fucking trou-trou-trouble. Nancy is so totally preoccupied with Ash's weight that I hoped she would want to be done with yelling at me as quickly as possible so she could raid the sugar stash under Ash's bed.

"Shut up!" Ash said.

"No, you shut up," I said back.

Nancy was standing in the hallway waiting for me. She pointed at Ash and said, "What have I said about that cursing, Ashley? You belong in bed, Little Miss Princess. And I had *better* not find any food under that bed when I come up in a few minutes."

Ash ignored our mother and remained standing at the door, through which some serious San Francisco Bay chill was whipping in.

"Close the door!" Josh yelled as he rode the stairway banister down into the hallway. "Burr-ito!"

"That's my expression," I reminded him. My expression via Shrimpilicious.

Sid-dad was nowhere to be seen, but I could smell his cigar wafting in from the study, his nightcap martini surely at his side.

"Thank you, Fernando," Nancy said, and she actually sounded like she meant it for once.

I was not going to thank Fernando. Not only did I introduce him to his new psychic advisor, Sugar Pie, but I personally didn't appreciate being hauled away from my brotherly Ocean Beach paradise by a big broody Nicaraguan who wouldn't even let us stop for donuts before he drove me back home.

Plus in the car, he told me how could I break my parents' hearts over and over again.

A lot Fernando knows.

"Are you happy, Cyd Charisse?" Nancy said as Josh and Ash ran around the hallway screaming and chasing one another. "Chaos reigns in this house, and once again you are the cause."

Uh, excuse me, but if I had been left in peace Chez Babe Brothers, this so-called chaos scene in the middle of the night would never have taken place.

"I am thinking about becoming legally emancipated," I announced. I am sixteen now and it is time we start talking seriously to one another, like adults. "You can expect a call from my lawyer in the morning."

I started to stroll up the stairs when I felt Nancy yank the back of my sweater to pull me back downstairs.

"That could be construed as child abuse in a court of law!" I snapped at her.

Nancy's face was all blotchy and furious when I turned around to face her. "I will not tolerate your fresh mouth any longer," she said, trying to stay calm.

"Little Hellion," Sid called from the study. "In here. Now."

I turned my cheek to Nancy, who followed me into the study.

Leila came to take my half-sibs back to bed. She shot me a look of pure hatred and for a second I almost felt bad. Leila hates to be woken up in the middle of the night. She has a hard time falling back asleep. I promised myself I would bring Leila some tea in bed after I dealt with the Sid and Nancy situation. I figured bedside tea service from an actual almost-waitress like myself was the least I could do for Leila.

I stood before Sid, who was actually wearing a smoking jacket as he smoked his cigar. I had to admire his style.

He was giving me a look of such disappointment I had to look away from him. I looked past him to the bookcase filled with all his favorite memorabilia: framed pix of me, Josh, and Ash; his college baseball glove; and the trophy we won together for winning the father-daughter potato sack race at his company picnic a few years earlier. Next to the trophy was the baseball we always used to throw together when I was little and just getting used to our new home in San Francisco, before Josh and Ash were born. Back then, Sid-dad used to come home from work early to play catch with me and read books with me; later, when I played Little League, he sometimes sent Fernando to take me to his office after school, and then Sid-dad and I would go over to this park near his office and hit balls and play catch. You throw like a girl, he used to tease me. And I would always remind him, I am a girl.

"Da . . . ," I started to say, but he cut me off lickety-split.

"Sit down," he said. When I hesitated, he announced, *"Now!"* and my butt hopped onto the leather sofa like that, almost like it was separated from my body and had a mind of its own.

Nancy stood at the door, wiping her nose with a Kleenex and trying to choke back tears.

"I don't get what the big deal is," I said.

"That's right you don't," Sid said. "But it's a very big deal, spending the night at *that boy's.*"

"But we weren't even having sex!" I protested.

There is such a thing as being too helpful with giving out information.

Sid-dad is very bald, so blushes on his face appear very obvious. Almost-daughters who throw like girls aren't supposed to grow up and have sex.

Sid did not look me in the eyes when he said, "You were out without permission and when you promised your mother you'd be home by eleven. You have abused the new trust we have tried to place in you and shown nothing but contempt for our good faith in you."

Good faith wha? I crossed over my leg and dangled my ankle around before announcing, "I've spent the night there before and you've never noticed or cared."

There was a silence in the room that felt good. My pronouncement was news to Sid and Nancy. They hadn't realized I had been sneaking in and out. I had gotten one over on them.

Fifteen

Apparently, I am no longer going to be getting one over on Sid and Nancy. Apparently, now they are going to notice everything I do, and they are going to care, big time.

I am grounded for, like, ever.

I can't work at Java the Hut any longer. I can see Sugar Pie once a week, but only because Fernando intervened and told Sid and Nancy they really need me at the home.

But now I have to spend as much time cleaning bathrooms at the home as I do visiting with Sugar Pie. Fernando's Revenge.

Oh, and now that I no longer have a job that pays me, I will not be able to afford that lawyer who might have taken care of the whole emancipation thing.

I am confined to this House Beautiful that looks like it should be a museum instead of a home where people live and breathe. From my room overlooking Pacific Heights and the Marina, I can see straight to the old prison island of Alcatraz. Did you know that prisoners who were marooned on Alcatraz could actually hear from their prison cells the voices of people in San Francisco laughing and having a good time, carried over by the strong Bay winds? I'm now calling my room Alcatraz. It is my desolate island where I can see people outside laughing and having a good time and I am sure they are all allowed to spend the night at their boyfriend's without being put on lockdown.

Everyone is walking around the house like it is a mortuary. Even the hyper-sibs are weirding out. Everyone is trying to be super nice to me, like they are afraid I will totally go postal in my new equation of 1 + Gingerbread = Alcatraz princess room. We're all whispering to each other and saying "please" and "thank you" all the time like we are strangers. After the night of screaming and slamming doors and tears, no one wants to break the peace.

I do. But I am biding my time.

Sid and Nancy have forbidden me to see Shrimp until the new school year starts. They said we all need a cooling-off period. I don't know what they are so afraid of. If they had any sense, they would know he is a dream boyfriend. And it's not like I am some vestal virgin. The headmaster from boarding school made sure they knew that. I guess Nancy likes to practice what they call "revisionist history" in my social studies class, because she is trying to lock me up like there is still something sacred left in me that's worth saving.

Josh and Ash are following me around the house like puppies. They are not used to me being home so much. But no amount of Josh doing Pee Wee Herman impressions or Ash braiding my hair and letting me use her Jell-O stomach for a pillow when we are watching videos can cheer me up.

I need a Shrimp.

I need a Wallace and stories of Australian-Indonesian lovers. I need Delia doing pliés all around the espresso machines.

I NEED A JAVA THE HUT COFFEE! BAD!

The only thing to do in Alcatraz is play Helen Keller. When I was little, Nancy used to read me this book all about how Helen was blind and deaf and survived like every obstacle to become this inspirational person. I would like to be an inspirational person, so late at night, when everyone is asleep and I would rather be snuggling up with Shrimp, I put a blindfold over my eyes and earplugs into my ears to drown out the sounds of the Bay winds, and I clutch Gingerbread to my heart and we walk around the puke princess room feeling the hard walls and pressing our cheeks against the cold window panes. Learning how to suffer without sight or sound will hopefully one day lead us down an inspirational path.

Helen was not mute but I am trying to be. I am not speaking to Nancy except when I have to. When we brush past each other in the mornings, I mumble, "Excuse me," and continue on my way. On my way to nowhere, that is, wandering around this huge boring house where Leila does not even care when I try to join her in the kitchen and explain to her the difference between a latte and a cappuccino. It's all about steamed versus foamed milk and the kind of drinking glass you use, I try to tell her, but she's all French-Canadian *Zut alors!* and she says, I have a job to do all day long, get out of the way.

Leila is furious at me because now Nancy is home all day long watching me like a hawk, which means she is in Leila's hair all day long, *Leila do this, Leila do that.* I offered Leila help to do this and that but she said, *Non.* I guess if I were Leila I would be mad at me too.

Only Gingerbread understands. She agrees that we are going to have to figure out a way to emancipate ourselves. We are thinking of adopting smoking habits, since that will at least occupy some of our time. Plus, smoking habits will really annoy Nancy.

Unfortunately, neither of us likes when our hair smells

like smoke, so we are trying to work out a compromise.

Gingerbread is having native urges. She wants to see real-dad, Frank.

Sid-dad has been coming home from work early, trying to coax me outside to barbecue with him or throw the baseball around. He wants me to "participate" in the family. I told him I'm not hungry and I don't like playing sports anymore, but thanks anyway. One time he came into my room with a special cappuccino he had bought on the way home for me. I asked, Is it a dry capp? and he said, Huh? and I said, You know, with extra foam and he said, Huh? and I said, I'm not really into coffee anymore either, but thanks. Again.

Nancy came into my room and said, "Are you going to grace us with your presence at dinner tonight, Miss I'm Too Good to Eat with My Family?"

"Sarcasm is as sarcasm does," I said back. *Forrest Gump* is Nancy's favorite movie. That tells you everything you need to know about my mother.

Nancy stood at the door to my room, not one hair out of place.

She sighed but didn't blow up. Prozac is really working for her, she really is trying. Calmly, she said, "Leila made your favorite, macaroni and cheese."

"Are you going to make Ashley eat grilled fish and rice, and not let her have dessert?" I asked.

"That's not your business," Nancy snapped back. "Ashley has a weight problem that could affect her socially. You will never understand. Not everybody is as metabolically blessed as you and can eat anything they want."

I was tempted to make a very crude comment about

certain male species nonfood items which I have metabolized, but Gingerbread shushed me.

"She's six," I said. "She should not be on a diet. And she is such a bossy girl that you don't have to worry about her at school. The kids in her school are all too scared *not* to be her friend."

I think it is pretty sad that my little sister wakes up in the middle of the night to sneak food from the fridge when she thinks everyone is sleeping because she is hungry from the dinner Nancy didn't let her finish. When I hear Ash late at night, I let her come into Alcatraz and we drink pretend tea from Gingerbread's tea set and eat mini-Nestlé Crunches. Then we jump on the bed and dance to mind-altering techno-pop to burn the cals even though we hate that kind of music.

Nancy said, "She's fifteen pounds overweight. That's extremely unhealthy for a six-year-old. You're not a parent, Miss Know-It-All. Don't tell me how to raise my child."

I'm not sure whether I hurt or help Ash's case by defending her to Nancy so I changed the subject. "I bet my real father would not imprison me like this," I said.

Nancy shook her head and I could tell she wanted to explode at me. Instead she said, "Be careful what you wish for," and walked away.

"Gingerbread and I will eat your LifeSavers for dinner!" I called after her.

I have to respect her for this. When Nancy rounded the corner and didn't think I could see her any longer, she flipped me the bird behind her back.

Sixteen

Just when I thought I was going to have to start a whole new sports game called Extreme Boredom, a miracle came into Alcatraz, thanks to my new best friend Delia.

Delia called my mom and said she was a part-time dance instructor at my high school, and she had noticed what a natural I was, and would Nancy consider enrolling me in her summer workshop at a little dance studio in Ocean Beach?

Well, Nancy said, she is grounded, but maybe this would be good for her. She's driving me nuts sulking all over the house. She was named for a famous dancer, you know.

The only problem was that Delia actually expected me to dance.

"Your name is Cyd Charisse!" she said when I arrived for my first lesson. "You have to learn how to dance!"

I was grateful that after dropping me off Fernando's Revenge had gone to the home so he could shoot dice with Sugar Pie and her pals. Having a gloomy Nicaraguan's glares melted by hysteria at watching me try to get jiggy on the studio dance floor would be too much to bear after my incarceration.

"Please don't tell me you want me to wear one of those leotards and wear leggings and act like some kind of dancer girl wannabe," I said to Delia.

"Someone has come to my little dance class with a bad attitude," Delia said. "Someone seems to have forgotten who sprung her from being grounded for the rest of the summer."

"Someone," I said, almost shouting, "HASN'T BEEN CAFFEINATED IN OVER A WEEK!"

Right on cue, Shrimp emerged from the dressing rooms carrying a hot double shot mocha with extra whipped cream, just the way I love. I didn't know whether to throw my arms around him or gulp first.

I chose the coffee. I have my priorities.

We all three sat on the giant wood floor, looking at our reflections in the giant mirrors. Delia was yammering on and on about tap versus modern for our first lesson, but I tuned her out to soak in Shrimp while I had the chance. I wanted to imprint into my memory every inch of his face and body to take back to the long days and nights in Alcatraz.

Shrimp sat by my side with the hint of a smile at the corners of his mouth. The platinum spike at the front of his head was a little longer and the roots darker than the last time I'd seen him, and his eyelashes, reflected in the afternoon sun peeking through the fog outside the dance studio windows, looked tinted with gold.

As the Java the Hut mocha with extra whip lushed its way through my bloodstream, I suddenly felt like I actually did want to dance. A zigzag combustible whoo-hoo freedom ride nas-tay kinda dance à la Shrimp 'n' Cyd aka porno Fred 'n' Ginger, and I wished Delia, cute as she was with her masses of orange frizzy hair piled on top of her head and her zebra-print tights, would ditch the joint.

Maybe I am just a sex maniac after all.

Shrimp had some whipped cream on his upper lip and

I just couldn't help myself. I leaned over to lick it off, but Shrimp looked into my eyes and knew what was on my mind. He quickly darted his eyes toward Delia and then turned his head to the side, so I wound up giving him an innocent eskimo kiss on the cheek.

That gesture sort of pissed me off.

What did he think I was going to do, bust a move on him right in front of Delia? He just looked so tasty and smelled like mountains of coffee beans, who could not want to lick him? But I am a proper girl and it would have been a proper lick.

"We have missed you at the coffeehouse!" Delia said. She babbled into espresso-fueled overdrive. "All the regulars are asking for you. We have a new girl working your hours named Autumn. Pretty girl but what a disaster! She can't figure out the espresso machine, breaks glasses all the time, always forgets customers' orders, but she's Shrimp's surfing friend and you know how Wallace likes to hire the kids from Ocean Beach."

I have not heard of this Autumn chick before from Shrimp. Cyd Charisse: not happy.

Suddenly I had a bad feeling about Shrimp being lick-free.

"You're not really going to make me dance around, are you?" I said. Maybe it was the sudden stimulation of being paroled from Alcatraz and drowned in coffee and Shrimpness after too bitter an absence, but I was getting a sudden caffeine headache. "Because I do not feel like dancing and all this coffee is making me want to pee."

Why I had to be mean and ornery when Delia and Shrimp were being so nice to me, I don't know.

"Dude," Shrimp said, "don't harsh my mellow."

"Well, why don't you go find Miss Autumn and have her un-harsh it for you!" I said. I stomped away to the bathroom.

While I sat on the toilet with my skirt around my ankles, I rested my elbows on my thighs and put my head in hands. I wanted to cry but all the five-minute insta-gulp coffee was making my hands shake so I couldn't concentrate enough to cry.

Autumn. AUTUMN?

"FUCK AUTUMN!" I yelled from the bathroom.

Autumn was probably some scraggly hippie chick with stringy red-gold hair and hairy armpits who carried around a guitar to strum stupid folk songs when she wasn't trying to be Miss Ocean Beach cool with her surfboard in one hand and Java the Hut latte in the other—decaf probably because of course she would want to maintain a totally mellow vibe at all times, dude. Wouldn't want Little Miss Autumn to harsh anyone's mellow while Cyd Charisse's Pieces is locked away in Alcatraz, breathing onto windows for entertainment.

When I returned from the bathroom, Delia was gone. Shrimp was staring out the huge windows looking as brooding as a Fernando wannabe.

"Where's Delia?" I asked.

"She thought we could use some time alone," he mumbled.

"But I wanted to learn how to dance!" I said. There was so much caffeine and sugar and head-pounding screaming for release in my body, I was ready to be the Lord of the Dance.

"Cyd," Shrimp said, so right away I knew we were not cool. He usually speaks my name silently, with longing in his eyes.

Some stupid reunion.

"We need to talk," Shrimp said.

Here's one superior feature of Justin's. He was not a sensitive Let's Talk About Our Feelings kind of guy. He was all sex, drugs, and rock 'n' roll. Sometimes that's a good thing.

"Talk about what?" I asked. I had to burn off the faux energy so I started to pace around the edges of the furnitureless dance studio.

"Us," Shrimp said.

"I can't believe you," I said. The coffee throttle was ready to be let loose from my mouth. "I finally get released from that hellhole called my mother's monster house and you want to 'talk.' Are you breaking up with me cuz if you are then (a) this is kind of a bad time to do it and (b) that is so totally lousy of you to bring me coffee first and be all sweet and fine-lookin' and then turn on me like that."

Math was my best subject at boarding school. The teacher said I excelled at deductive reasoning.

"*I'm* turning on *you?*" Shrimp said. "Hello! You're like a totally different person right now. You're like this dog Curl we adopted when I was a kid. Curl had been in a cage for months and was like this wild monster when he was first released. You're reminding me of Curl now. Your parents have really done a number on you while you've been grounded."

"At least my parents stick around!" I said back as I

paced. I instantly regretted my comeback but that's the thing about unkind words: You can try to undo the damage, but (a) it's hard when you're all coffee-ed up, and (b) you can't take it back, ever.

Shrimp's shoulders went into a slouch and he stopped following my pace with his eyes. It was like a tide change so fast we could have evaporated into the Ocean Beach fog rolling in thick and thunderous outside the windows.

How had our reunion gone so wrong, so fast?

There was a silence that lasted too long, broken only by the hard taps of my pounds around the dance floor. When Shrimp finally spoke, he said, "Be still for a minute, would you? You're making me dizzy with all that pacing."

I stopped exactly in front of him. In my sudden stillness, I wanted to etch his face and smell into the memory which I knew was about to be all I would have left of Shrimp. I touched the platinum spike on his hair, then closed my eyes and pretended I was Helen Keller. Helen molded her hands into Shrimp's cheeks and eyes, his lips and nose, to forever retain the shape of him.

"So what now?" I asked, my eyes still closed. The silence had been so nice, but I couldn't play deaf forever.

Shrimp said, "This separation has gotten me thinking. We've been hanging out so much since we met that I've hardly had time to finish a canvas or see my surfing friends or anything. I wasn't sure until just now, but maybe us being apart for a while is a good thing. Maybe your parents aren't as dumb as you think."

"Do you love me?" I whispered.

When Shrimp didn't answer, I let my hands fall to my sides and opened Helen's eyes to the mean bitter world.

It was like he didn't even hear my question. Shrimp said, "I didn't realize till you were gone how much we've been crowding each other. I need some time and space for my surfing and painting, you know?"

"And for Autumn?" I said. I looked straight into his beauty eyes so he would know he couldn't lie to me.

"There's nothing between me and Autumn," he said, not looking straight back at me.

"You just lied to Helen!" I said. The eyes gave him away.

"Huh?" Shrimp said.

"So this is it then?" I asked. Cuz for weeks in Alcatraz I had been hanging on to the time when I could see Shrimp again, touch him, laugh with him. Not fight with him. Certainly not break up with him. *Especially* not be tweaked by an Autumn.

"We'll see each other when the school year starts. We'll figure this out then."

Right.

As he stepped outside, he turned back once and mumbled, "And maybe you need some time to figure out your crush on my brother."

Then he walked out of the studio and into the fog and I closed my eyes so Helen wouldn't have to witness this final horribleness.

"I thought you were forever," Helen said to his dark shadow.

Seventeen

The new Helen Keller commune is now in session in
Alcatraz. It is the speak-no-evil-see-no-evil-hear-no-evil
commune.

We allow new people in only by scent. People who
smell like the perfume ladies at Neiman Marcus are out. So
sadly Nancy will not be joining us. Martinis and Cuban
cigars are always nice to smell, but Sid-dad has not sub-
mitted an application for membership. Nicaraguans who
smell of empanadas and morning church services might be
allowed in if they ask nice. Who doesn't love the smell of
sweets? Sugar Pie and your chocolate collection, always
glad to have you in the new Helen Keller commune.

There is no need to invite Blank—he whose name
hurts too much to even think so that it's good we don't have
to speak it or picture him (seeing as how we're deaf and
blind). Blank's brother Java would make an aromatic addi-
tion to our commune but we can't risk choking on tears by
asking him or Delia and then potentially being tempted to
ask about Blank. I have telepathically invited Lucinda,
Wallace's former Australian-Indonesian love, and she mes-
saged back: "Gerr-ate!" She knows what it is like to pine
and hurt for and be dumped by a beautiful surfer punk-
dude.

Ash and Josh, who always smell of chocolate-chip
cookies and mischief, are charter members of the Helen
Keller commune. Every day we wander around the Who

Cares If It's a House Beautiful Cuz We Can't See It with blindfolds over our eyes and earplugs in our ears. Management unfortunately moved us to the basement after we broke too many vases, but in the basement commune of Helen Keller we can jump on trampolines and not care if we fall and hurt ourselves because we are together and that makes us happy.

Soon I am going to have to tell Ash and Josh about our prospective new members, Rhonda and Daniel, my other half-sibs. Just because Rhonda and Daniel are a little old for playing Helen Keller commune doesn't mean they won't. I am their sister, their blood, and even if they can't see me or hear me, they can feel me. I know it.

Eighteen

Sometimes playing Helen Keller when you are not actually blind or deaf is not an effective way to not think about being dumped by a Shrimp or the fact that you are dying of boredom and sadness and yearning for something, anything, to change, to make life interesting and exciting again, even when you are grounded into eternity.

I was wandering around the house after Ash and Josh had gone to "sleep" when I came outside the door to Sid-dad's study.

Nancy was saying, "I can't take Miss Moping anymore. She's driving me nuts."

Driving *you* nuts? Hell-oh! Try driving *me* nuts.

Sid said, "So, do you want to let her go? Because much as I missed the hell out of her when she was at boarding school, this grounding experiment is clearly not working. Everyone in the house is miserable. Maybe it's time the Little Hellion learned to appreciate the people who love and care for her in this family, and sending her you-know-where might be the best way to accomplish that."

I pulled the earplugs out so I could hear better. This was too much. I knew Nancy and I were not getting along, but I never thought she would want to kick me out over it! And wherever You-Know-Where was, I so was not going. But if I had to run away, then where would I go? Not to Shrimp. Maybe to Wallace. That would show Shrimp. I could have Wallace in a minute if I wanted.

But there are certain lines even I know better than to cross.

The only place I would really want to go is to New York. To Frank real-dad's. It is like the body of Cyd Charisse is one big jigsaw puzzle, with pieces picturing Shrimp (mean boy); Sugar Pie; Ash and Josh; Alcatraz; Gingerbread, of course; Fernando and Leila; and Sid and Nancy. But the pieces are all scattered and can only be put together properly if I can find the pictures with the Empire State Building, Rhonda and Daniel, and my real father.

Still, it did not feel nice to know that Nancy wanted me gone. I would never want my baby to leave me.

Nancy said, "Maybe it's time. This family will not survive the summer with all this tension. And as much as I hate to throw her to wolves like that, maybe getting to know Frank—God help her—will be a good thing for her. Allow her to move on."

Yo! My mother wanted to send me to the one place where I wanted to go! The thought that my mother might be psychic made me practically nauseous.

"So we're settled then?" Sid-dad said. I could hear a faint tinge of sadness in his voice.

Nancy's voice wavered just a little. "I guess. You'll call Frank in the morning?"

"I will," Sid-dad said, then laughed. "Old Frankie boy doesn't know what he set himself up for when he asked to spend some time with the Little Hellion. The King of the

New York Advertising World is about to get himself a little lesson in humility."

I think Sid-dad was paying me a compliment, but I'm not sure.

I raced back to Alcatraz to tell Gingerbread the news.

I jumped on the bed, excited about something for the first time since I got a job at Java the Hut, which was only like eight weeks ago but seemed like lifetimes ago. "We're going to New York, Gingerbread! Going to New Yorkie York, and we are going to see Frank and meet Rhonda and Daniel and we are going to ride the subway and feel the grunge and wear black every single day and we are not going to miss Shrimp AT ALL!"

Gingerbread smiled back. Sometimes she reminds me of Mrs. Butterworth and I can tell she is about to open up her arms to offer me a hug or some syrup.

I was still jumping when I heard a knock on the door so I fell onto the bed and shouted, "COME IN!" I attached a frown to my face so Nancy wouldn't be too weirded out by my sudden excitement.

"You don't need to yell," Nancy said. "The kids are sleeping."

As if. On my way back to my room I saw Ash and Josh playing War with a flashlight under his bed. But I decided to be nice and not point out that fact. Sometimes it's better to let Nancy live in the fantasy world where we're one big, happy, quiet family.

"Oh, sorry," I whispered.

"Why are you out of breath?" Nancy asked. She actually had color in her face, maybe because Sid had given Leila the night off and grilled steaks and veggies for dinner and Nancy had actually eaten.

"Dunno," I said, trying to contain the smile that was ready to burst out of my lips.

Nancy sat next to me on the puke princess bed. Then she did a shocker. She picked up Gingerbread and placed my doll on her lap. Gingerbread was good; she didn't squirm.

"I think it's pretty obvious that neither you nor I is happy with the current situation in this house," Nancy said.

One thing I like about Nancy is that she doesn't mess around getting to her point. None of that "we need to talk" business.

I wanted to be extra nice because Nancy was holding her sometimes-nemesis, Gingerbread, so I said, "I could try harder."

Nancy actually laughed! Then she leaned over a little and played with my hair.

"I know you could, sweetie. I guess I could too." Nancy paused and then she said, "Are we actually having a conversation that doesn't involve yelling or cursing?"

"Let's not push it," I said.

"Right," Nancy said. "You've always wanted to meet your biological father. Well, I have a lot of misgivings about this, but if you are ready, then I am willing. His wife passed away last year and he has been in touch with Sid and me and would like to have you visit, to get to know you. What do you think about that?"

"Sure," I mumbled. To Gingerbread, I telepathed, "YEAH!"

My real-dad was a widower. Tragedy about to be

remedied by the arrival of one Cyd Charisse, hellion daughter extraordinaire.

Nancy said, "Maybe some time in New York will help you not think about *that boy,* the surf stalker."

"It's slacker, Mom, not stalker," I said.

"Right," Nancy said. *"That boy."* She waited, I guess thinking I might give her information as to whether *that boy* and I had managed to communicate during my Alcatraz incarceration. She waited.

"Well, do you want to go?" Nancy said. "I could come with you if you want."

My adventure in New York with Frank real-dad, and did I want Nancy trotting along? Hell, no!

"No, thank you," I said.

Even prisoners know how to be polite.

Nineteen

I was so nervous to meet Frank real-dad again that I actually broke out into a sweat when the plane landed in New York. Even Gingerbread was nervous. I could practically feel her bouncing on my lap.

"Aren't you a little old for dolls?" this creepmeister executive man sitting next to me in first class said. The whole flight he had been pretending not to stare at Gingerbread, who had been sitting on my black tights, right below my short skirt, during the flight.

"Aren't *you?*" I said back.

Creepmeister executive man did not try to help me with my luggage in the overhead bin.

Since I didn't have a star student report card or Homecoming Queen tiara to impress Frank real-dad, I had brought him real gingerbread that I had baked myself, without Leila's help. It was kind of crumbly but it smelled ginger 'n' cloves yumster under the red bowtie-wrapped tinfoil. Gingerbread-doll was not upset by my baking efforts; it wasn't like when you go to a farm for the day and make friends with cows that you know will be steak one day. She understood the difference between namesake and food chain.

So there I was, strolling into the arrival area at the airport, carrying Gingerbread-doll and hoping gingerbread-cake would stay together until I could present it to Frank real-dad, but of course I tripped on the strings which had come loose on my four-inch platform combat boots, and *splat* I went. *Smoosh* went gingerbread-cake, flying went Gingerbread-doll, *mortificado* went Cyd Charisse's Pieces. I saw my usually chalk-white face in a mirror as I stood up, and it was the color of a tomato.

"You Cyd?" said this guy who sounded like John Travolta. He extended his hand to my shoulder to steady me. His other hand was carrying a sign with my name on it. He was like New York Knicks tall with Puerto Rican honey eyes and luscious cinnamon skin. A certain boy whose name rhymes with chimp, limp, and gimp was the farthest Blank from my mind. Let me just say, even if my name hadn't been Cyd, I'd have been like, "You betcha!"

"How did you know that?" I asked as I scrambled to pick up Gingerbread.

He had this insane-sexy New York accent. You could practically hear him saying, "yo!" and "youz guys" every other beat. He said, "You look just like Frank. No way you could be anyone besides his niece. He sent me here to pick you up. I'm Luis. I work for Frank. We'll be seeing a lot of each other these next couple weeks."

"His *niece?*" I said. I picked up gingerbread-cake and tossed it in the trash.

Twenty

Maybe Frank suspected our weird resemblance, and that's why he didn't come pick me up at the airport himself. Maybe he was scared to see me, scared that he would fall totally in love with his new daughter and never be able to send me back to my family in San Francisco, and that's why he made me wait with Luis at his apartment for hours and hours until he came home from work. I couldn't help but compare: Sid-dad had taken the day off work to personally drive me to the airport (he said it was because Fernando was still mad at me but we both knew it was because he was going to miss his Little Hellion) and to lecture me in the car about, like, always wearing a hat in the sun, and trying to find a place in my heart to get along with Nancy, and how I shouldn't let anyone make a Yankees fan out of me when he'd spent years making me a Red Sox fan, and yet Frank-dad couldn't even be bothered to pick me up at the airport, much less hang with me my first hours in Nuevo York.

Not like waiting with Luis (or "Loo-eese" as he says it . . . sigh) was such trauma city. Luis and I clicked like buds right away, starting from the moment when I ignored the back door to the Town Car he held open for me and I hopped into the front seat.

"You're a frontie, eh?" Luis said, smiling.

"Nah," I said. "I am just from Cali, where we are more laid-back."

"It's like that?" said Luis dream-driver (Fernando, take notes).

My deductive reasoning instinct kicked in and I said, "Suppose you had to pick me up in the middle of the night for something, okay, and—"

"Uh-oh, you're in trouble already?"

"I most certainly am not. You didn't let me finish. Suppose you had to pick me up in the middle of the night. Would you stop for donuts if I asked?"

Luis thought on it a second and said, "Krispy Kremes or Dunkin' Donuts?"

"Either," I said, even though the correct answer was Dunkin' Donuts.

"Krispy Kremes, yes. Dunkin' Donuts, no."

There's no accounting for taste, as Nancy says.

I still loved Luis anyway. I was trying to figure out if his sweat-clinged T-shirt muscle mania biceps could possibly be any sexier.

"How come it is so hot here?" I asked, leaning in to blast the a/c.

"It's August! Whadja expect?"

"I did not expect to be sweltering," I said. "In San Francisco in the summer you have to wear a winter coat."

"Get out!" Luis said.

"It's true." I nodded.

When we drove into the city, I was surprised that I did not remember it at all. I was born in New York, but it did not feel like a homecoming when I saw those massive skyscrapers. The skyline looked like a sci-fi madness kingdom.

"Did Frank tell you about me?" I asked Luis.

"No," Luis said. "He just gave me your flight information."

I had the feeling Luis was used to not asking Frank for personal details.

"Well, I am not his niece," I said.

"No kidding." Luis laughed.

I guess I had always imagined Frank living in a big mansion in the country somewhere with like a huge dog who slobbered onto ancient carpets and framed photographs of Rhonda and Daniel on tables and walls everywhere, pictures chronicling from the time they were buck-teethed babes to their high school graduations, with bad hair and big grins. Maybe there would be a wall in the family room marked with crayon lines to show how much Rhonda and Daniel grew every year, like the kind Ash, Josh, and I made in a closet in the basement because Nancy would freak if we touched her upstairs interior decorated walls. So I was surprised to arrive at a condo on the Upper East Side of Manhattan that was totally the bachelor dude kind of pad. There were two bedrooms in the apartment, with big dining and living rooms overlooking Central Park, but the furniture was all leather and corporate-y: new. I had hoped I would get to sleep in Rhonda's old room and I could go through her old yearbooks and read her diary or something, but instead Luis showed me to a guest bedroom that had as much character as a glass of milk. And what good is plain milk without a shot of espresso? The hotel-looking furniture needed a serious splash of leopard print. Suddenly Alcatraz seemed like a resort in comparison to The Real Dad Corporate Suites.

"There's a big TV in the living room," Luis offered. I think he could tell how disappointed I was by the bland twenty-seventh-floor condo shimmering in the sky.

"I don't like TV," I said.

"Did you say you're sixteen?" Luis asked, to which I wanted to respond, "Not too young for you!" but I just nodded my head.

"You don't like any of them TV shows about girl witches and such?" Luis continued.

"What shows?" I said.

Luis look at me suspiciously and said, "What are they feeding you in San Francisco?"

"Food," I answered. Dim sum with Blank, chocolate with Sugar Pie, black coffee for Fernando, Twinkies for Ash and gummi bears for Josh, martinis and steaks for Sid-dad, and for Nancy, ye olde LifeSavers.

In my Helen Keller commune, I had imagined that from the second I arrived in New York, my life would be different. Changed. Instead, I felt uncomfortable and scared, a stranger in a strange land. I clutched Gingerbread for support.

"A sixteen-year-old girl with a doll?" Luis said.

"Yes."

There was a pause like Luis was waiting for me to explain. Finally he said, "Hey, I'm cool with that," and I could tell, Gingerbread was feeling the crush power, too.

The sun had gone down and there was a red twilight glow over Central Park while Luis and I played Scrabble. I was just about to slay him with a triple word score "LOLLI" to add to his "POP" when Frank arrived home.

He put his briefcase down and said, "How do, kiddo?"

He did not open his arms to me and anyway that would have been weird if he did. I was still sitting at the table as I looked at him. There was a frog in my throat. Suddenly I understood why the sight of me pains Nancy. If my baby was a 24/7 physical reminder of Justin, that would break my heart over and over again. Luis had not been kidding about me looking just like my "uncle."

Frank had slick, ink black hair with specks of gray; wide eyes; big red lips; and a long, straight nose just like mine. The only difference between us was that he was orange-tan from what looked like a tanning booth and not some Caribbean paradise, and I am fog-dweller pale. Plus from the lines around his eyes, I suspected his face produced smiles much more than mine. When I stood up to shake his hand, he was one of the first men I have ever met who was significantly taller than me.

Frank was also ridiculously handsome. Does that make me a skank for noticing that? Because he totally had the older man retired movie star thing going on. My heart dropped for Nancy again; if I had been twenty years old and not known better (even though I do, and I am only sixteen), I could understand how some dancer girl with stars in her eyes straight from the Minnesota cornfields could have fallen for his white teeth, sparkling eyes, and smooth lies.

I think even Frank was tweaked by our resemblance. He kept staring at me like he was thinking, *Oh . . . my . . . god.* Finally he said, "You must be tired from your flight."

Huh? Here I am your new long-lost all-grown-up daughter, and the best you have to say is, "You must be tired from your flight"? *Como se dice?*

"Not really," I said. I was so *not* tired after the pre-Scrabble venti Starbucks run (Java be damned) with Luis that I wouldn't have minded snaring Luis to go salsa danc-ing all night but for my big reunion with my biological father and all. No biggie, right?

Because it seemed to me that Frank real-dad had a lot of explaining to do, and now was as good a time as any to get started.

Twenty-one

What better way to get started, I thought, than by announcing to Frank: "I am not your niece, you know."

Before Frank could so much as reply, Luis jumped up, knocking over the Scrabble game. He grabbed his phone and said to Frank, "I'm outta here. Call me you need anything." And *poof!* like that Loo-eese was gone. I gave Gingerbread a look so she wouldn't pout.

Once the door had closed behind him, Frank paused for a moment, as if he didn't know how to respond. Then he said, "Whoa there, pardner! Give a person a chance to settle in."

"'Whoa there, pardner'?" I asked.

"It's a saying," he said.

"On what planet?"

Frank sighed. Only two minutes into my reunion with Frank real-dad, and already I had exasperated him. I suspected this time was a new personal best for me.

"Are you hungry?" he finally said.

Since I figured maybe after a good meal he would be more likely to tell me the important details about, like, everything—my family history on his side, how he came to know my mom, where had he been all my life, who was he, really?—I figured it was easier to let him off the hook for the time being.

"I am so always hungry," I told him. Which is true. If I'm not hungry for food, then I'm hungry for something bigger: answers to the secrets of the universe, true love, a more substantial bustline.

Frank real-dad's shoulders seemed to relax a little, like me being hungry was something he could actually deal with, part of the known universe that was Cyd Charisse, progeny.

"Well, all right then." He placed his briefcase on the Scrabble table and walked past me toward the kitchen. He was careful not to stare at me like I was staring at him. He smelled like cigars and martinis, like Sid-dad. I wanted to shout at him: HALT! Stand before me and let me look at you. Let me understand who you are. Let's make this connection NOW. Even though I was supposed to spend three weeks with him, I still wanted time to freeze, so I could soak in everything about him, before he disappeared again like he had when I was five, at the Dallas-Fort Worth Airport, when he gave me Gingerbread.

I followed him into the kitchen and he handed me a stack of delivery menus for a rainbow coalition of foods: Thai, Chinese, Malaysian, soul food, pizza, Vietnamese, Texas BBQ, Mexican, Irish pub, Jewish deli, Greek diner. Each menu offered food Nancy would never let into her fat-free, sugar-free, taste-free House Beautiful, and bonus, most of the restaurants delivered until about three in the morning. I thought of the C-spots Sid-dad had snuck into my handbag at the airport in San Francisco and was psyched that if I woke up starving in the middle of the night (which, since Blank dumped me, happened a LOT), that I could order yum food and not have to ask Frank for money and not have to worry about Leila complaining in the morning about how I messed up her kitchen.

"What'll it be, kiddo?" Frank said after I had salivated over the menus for probably ten whole minutes, during which time Frank had turned on the stereo and was now blasting Frank Sinatra, that good lookin', smooth soundin' "Chairman of the Board," as Sid-dad says. Sid-dad thinks Francis Albert Sinatra, born December 12, 1915, in Hoboken, New Jersey, and died May 15, 1998, whose birthday our household is forced to celebrate and whose death we mourn every year, is the sun around which we mere earthlings revolve.

"What's with the 'kiddo' thing?" I asked. "My name is Cyd Charisse."

"Your mother chose that name," Frank grumbled, like he was embarrassed by the name.

"I think it's a nice name," I said. Who ever thought I would enter a zone where I would defend a choice of Nancy's? I'm actually impartial to my name. It is what it is: mine, and that dancer movie star's. "Even if I am not a dancer person and even if when I say my name people say back, 'Oh, and I'm Greta Garbo,' or 'Oh, and I'm Grace Kelly.'"

"Grace Kelly," Frank real-dad said, "now *she* was a looker."

What-ever, dawg!

I made my dinner choice and handed Frank the menu for Miss Loretta's House of Great Eats. Frank laughed. "Why is that funny?" I asked.

"Because you chose the one restaurant from over a dozen menus that is run by our friend Loretta Jones. She used to be our housekeeper. My son and I helped her start this business."

I instantly made the connection. "She made the ginger-bread!" I exclaimed.

"Well, yes, gingerbread is her specialty . . ."

". . . no, she made the gingerbread that time . . ."

". . . what time?"

"The time at the airport in Dallas-Fort Worth. She made the gingerbread!" This was like the most exciting thing ever but Frank cast his eyes down, ashamed.

"Well, yes," he stammered, "if I was carrying ginger-bread she had probably made it. Loretta's an amazing cook." Frank was clearly embarrassed and I could feel Gingerbread's annoyance vibes psychically floating back from the living room where she was presiding over the knocked-over Scrabble board. "What would you like to eat?"

"Can we go eat there? At Miss Loretta's restaurant?"

"No," Frank said hurriedly. When he saw how disap-pointed my face was, he added, "Well, maybe sometime soon. Not tonight."

Gingerbread and I had had it. I crossed my arms across my chest and said, "You mean not until you've told Miss Loretta that I'm not your niece and that I'm really your bio-logical daughter from when you were cheating on your wife?"

"You don't mince words, do you, Cyd Charisse?" Frank asked. He was uncomfortable but I think he was a little impressed, too.

I jumped up to sit on the bar ledge. "Let's be real, Frank," I said, knocking my boots against the backboard. In the Alcatraz days before I left for New York, I had imagined that Frank and I would form an instant father-daughter connection, that I would call him "Daddy" and he would call me "Princess" or some such, but that was obviously not going to happen and anyway, now that I was seeing what he was like, I didn't think he was the type of person I would feel comfortable calling "Dad."

"Frank, I am not your niece. I am your biological daughter. Deal with it. If you are embarrassed by me, say so right now and I will go somewhere else." I don't know what I was thinking because really I had nowhere else to go and I wanted more than anything in the whole stupid world to get to know this strange person standing in front of me, but at the same time, I didn't want to be in a place where I was not welcome.

Frank hopped up onto the bar next to me. "Ouch," he said. "That hurt." I didn't know whether he meant the pain from heaving his old guy body up onto the bar or from what I had said. He paused and then turned sideways to look at me. "You're right, kiddo—I mean, Cyd. This whole situation is very awkward and new to me. I'm a sixty-year-old man with two adult children and now a new sixteen-year-old daughter. I've made a lot of mistakes in my life and not always comported myself in a manner I'm proud of. I'm new to all this—will you help me out here?"

I was still mad and for sure had never heard the word "comported" before but I said, "Okay," because what if he was a sixty-year-old man who had made a lot of mistakes but then all of a sudden dropped dead from a heart attack after the smothered chicken with cornbread, mashed potatoes, and apple pie dinner I was intending to order, and I hadn't said I would try? I don't think I could have lived with that.

"You're pretty together, you know that, Cyd Charisse?"

Frank said. "To hear your mother and Sid tell it, you're hell on wheels."

Like that made sense.

"I think it's time to order, Frank. I'm not letting you off about meeting Miss Loretta, but let's just order in tonight. Anyways, I think there are some girl witch shows we need to watch on TV tonight."

Frank real-dad smiled. If I ever smiled, I'd say my smile looks just like his.

Twenty-two

So maybe Frank and I had near-bonded over a girl witch show and Miss Loretta's amazing chicken dinner, but when I woke up at noon the next day (which Nancy would never have let happen, even if I had been kept awake all night by Chinese water torture or something), Frank was gone. There was a note on the fridge that said, "Luis will be by after lunchtime to show you around. I'll be home by ten tonight— business dinner. The doorman downstairs has the apartment keys for you. Have fun, Cyd Charisse. —F." There was a $50 bill attached to the note which I ripped off the fridge, stuffed down the garbage disposal, and obliterated to shreds.

Then I remembered how Sugar Pie said I have a rich person's conceit and I felt guilty for wasting money like that. Even if I was mad and didn't want Frank's money, I could have at least given it back to him or given it to a poor person who really needed it. I decided to call Sugar Pie and confess. Guess who answered her telephone? Fernando! I looked down at the Mickey Mouse watch on my wrist that Blank had given me for Valentine's Day. He had painted the straps in this psychedelic tie-dye pattern that made Mickey look like a freak. According to the Mickey Freak, who was still on Cali time, it was just past Sugar's breakfast hour.

"*Huevos rancheros* for two?" I asked Fernando, forgetting all about my confession. There was a silence and I knew Fernando was trying for me not to know he was happy to hear my voice. I also knew Fernando was mortified so I decided to be discreet. "May I please speak with Sugar?"

There was a pause and then Sugs' voice replied, "Good morning, baby. How was your trip?"

"It was okay. Gingerbread and I think New York is too hot. My hair is all curly and wild here. So are you and Fernando a couple now because that would be the coolest if you were and don't you know that younger guys are totally hip." Blank is six months younger than me, but a full grade behind.

Sugar Pie said, "A lady never tells."

"Don't be a lady," I said. Sugar Pie didn't say anything back. She wasn't giving up the dope. I continued, "Fernando is kind of cool but don't tell him I said that, 'kay? I am still mad at him for dragging me away from you-know-where in the middle of the night and starting all this trouble."

"You know that wasn't his fault. You know whose fault that was. You know he was just doing his job."

"Mmmm," I said. I wanted so much to ask if she had seen Blank and if he was hurting for me or even asking about me. Did he know I'd gone to New York to meet Frank real-dad? Did he know Loo-eese was a threat to him?

"Yes, your boy has poked around a few times the last week, if that's what you really want to know." Sugar Pie would be psychic even without her tarot cards.

"Was there some lame chick called Autumn with him?" I asked.

"Autumn? Who's Autumn?"

That response made me feel a little better. At least Blank wasn't dragging HER along to visit with MY people. I asked Sugar, "Do you think he misses me?"

Sugar Pie said, "What do you think, Cyd Charisse?"

"What kind of answer is that?" I asked.

"Missy, you're in the most exciting city in the world supposed to be having all kinds of new adventures. Maybe the answer you don't want to accept is what you already know. Sometimes you need to lose a person to find yourself. Sometimes only then can you get that person back. Make sense?"

"No, Obi-wan," I said.

"You'll figure it out. We miss you here but don't expect to see you back till you've figured some things out, seen something of the world. Now get off the phone and go explore."

"Don't you want to know about my real dad?" I asked.

Sugar said, "I've read your cards. I already know. Now stop wasting your life and go outside and have some fun. But BE CAREFUL."

I didn't want to let her hang up—what was I supposed to do all alone in this sci-fi twenty-seventh-floor condo thingie with honking horns and people swarming around fast-fast-fast everywhere outside? But on the other hand, I wanted Sugar Pie to enjoy her time with Fernando. I know how much I hated to be interrupted when Blank and I were alone.

"Okay, bye." I was about to hang up, then added, "I love you, Sugar." I realized I could toss those words out like Mardi Gras beads to Sugar Pie, but you would not catch me dead saying those words to Nancy.

"You too, baby. Have fun. Call me after you have some adventures to report."

"Kisses to Fernando!" I said. Sugar let out a whopping laugh at that comment and hung up.

I looked around the apartment and didn't know what to do. All those weeks locked up in Alcatraz, and now I had all the freedom in the world in the city that doesn't sleep, and I was paralyzed. There seemed to be too much possibility. I took Gingerbread in my arms and turned on the tube. There was a public access program of these Indian women wearing beautiful saris doing some kind of sari-ness dance. It was quite spectacular looking and Gingerbread and I joined in, as if we were participating in an exercise program for our morning workout. I was all into head swishes and hip-to-hand tra-la-la when I heard the sound of applause coming from behind me. Figuring it must be Loo-ese, I curved the ends of my lips upward and turned around to say "Hey . . . ," but it was not Loo-eese standing before me. Standing in front of me wearing a T-shirt that was actually gray but said "BROWN" on it was a mini-Frank. Well, not literally a mini-Frank but a much younger, thinner, and somewhat shorter version of bio-dad.

I knew who he was—did he know who I was?

"You must be Cyd Charisse," mini-Frank said.

"I know who you are, too. You're Daniel!"

He looked a little quizzical and said, "Did Dad tell you that's my name? The only time I get called that is at, like, graduations and doctor's offices."

"Do you have a totally cute nickname like Junior or Flash or Poncho?" I asked.

He looked even more confused and said, "No, charm girl. People just call me Danny."

I jumped up onto the sofa—I have no idea why—to reach and shake Danny's hand on the other side of the sofa. "You can call me Cyd or Cyd Charisse. Sid is also the name of my other dad so's people at home call me by both names but here in Manhattan I am like starting a whole new identity so you could use my real name or even make one up if you want."

"Loving you, lil' sis!" Danny singsonged. He was too adorable. He came around to my side of the sofa and jumped up on it next to me to shake my hand. "Pleased to meet you, secret love child."

"That's not the nickname you want to use for me, is it?"

Danny smiled and said, "No, Cyd Charisse. When I think of a good one for you, I'll let you know."

I wanted to know, "You're not mad or anything about my being here?" Looking into his eyes was like looking into a mirrored reflection of my own: the same dark brown color; his hair was the same dark black as mine, his lips the same full ruby red. The difference between looking at him and Frank real-dad was that with Danny I felt an instant *ka-pow!* connection. When I looked at Frank and saw our resemblance, I felt distant—separated from myself—and a little betrayed, and not at all comfortable. With my other family in San Francisco, even though Josh looks just like Nancy (he is totally the handsome Prince William babe-in-training) and Ash takes after Sid-dad and I look like the answer to the "what is wrong with this picture" question in our family portraits, at least I know more or less where I belong in that family.

Danny said, "Mad? No! How could I be mad at you about something you had nothing to do with." He plopped down onto the sofa into a sitting position and gestured me to join him. Way weirdness—once sitting on the sofa, we both crossed our legs Indian style at the same exact time.

"I've known about you for years and have been dying to see you! Daddy finally told me about you last week—I tried to act surprised—but I couldn't wait for him to introduce us. I've always wanted a little sister."

"I've always wanted to be one!" I exclaimed.

"Then we're a match!" Danny said. How funny that in my imagination he was some macho tough football dude, but live and in the flesh I could see he was just a regular Joe kinda fella who wore his heart on his sleeve.

"Is Rhonda coming to meet me too?" I asked. Because that would be the final chapter, of course, when my big sister and I became Sisters like in that song from the movie *White Christmas* although we probably wouldn't wear matching outfits and sing together, although we would totally read each other, like, instinctually.

"Rhonda?" Danny said. "Daddy told you our sister's name was Rhonda?"

I didn't want to explain how I read about them in a book and how Frank and I still had not touched the subject of me meeting his other children so I just said, "Not exactly."

Danny said, "My sister uses her middle name. Rhonda was an old family name. She never goes by that."

"Then what is her name and is she coming to see me too?"

Danny's face turned down and he said, "Lisbeth is having a little bit of a harder time with this. But she'll come around."

When he pronounced her name, he said the "Lis" part really fast and the "Beth" part really hard and long: lisBETH. It was the kind of stupid name some fourteen-year-old girl adopts when she is writing in a diary and if she keeps the name when she is an adult, she most likely has problems.

"Oh," I said and I looked to the ceiling so he would not be able to tell that tears wanted to form in my eyes. "Does she not like me?"

"How can she not like you? She doesn't even know you," Danny answered.

You'd think! "Then why isn't she here with you?"

Danny said, "Lisbeth is . . . ," Danny paused, searching for the right word, "special. She can come across as very angry and rigid, but once you get to know her, you'll see that she's all right. She always has the best of intentions."

If ever there was a warning flare, that was it. I figured the lisBETH issue was for a later time. For the here and now, I wanted to get to know Danny, the sweetest older brother ever.

"So, can we like hang out and stuff? I have nothing to do!" I told him.

Danny looked at his watch. "I have to be back at work in half an hour . . ."

"What do you do?" I interrupted.

"I'm a baker and cake decorator."

"No!" I said, awed. The thought of all his sugar access on top of my just finishing a conversation with my Sugar felt like fate or something. "That would quite possibly have to be the coolest job ever. Do you decorate wedding cakes or naughty cakes?"

Danny grinned and said, "I dabble with both. My partner and I own a little café down in the West Village. He does the cooking and I do the baking and we also do catering for special events like weddings and parties and things like that."

I could tell he watched my face closely when he said the word "partner" to see how I would react.

"Is your boyfriend as cute as you and does he want to meet me too?" I asked.

I could see there was an unspoken test that I had just passed in Danny's eyes. "Yeah, Aaron wants to meet you too. Why don't you come down to the café a little later this afternoon after we've got everything ready for the evening crowd?"

"Cool!" I said. "Should I ask Luis to drive me?" How much did I want to call Blank and tell him that both our older brothers owned cafés? More than a lot. If ever there was cosmic evidence that we were soulmates, here it was. But I plucked the thought from my brain and told it buh-bye.

"Drive!" Danny exclaimed. "Nobody drives in Manhattan!"

Confused, I said, "But Frank told me Luis . . ."

"Oh, Daddy," Danny said. "He probably assumed Uncle Sid has a driver take you everywhere, so he is being competitive." Danny rolled his eyes.

"*Uncle* Sid?" I asked. "You know my dad?"

"Know your dad? He's my godfather. He and Daddy were roommates at Harvard; they were best friends for years, until the falling out over you and Uncle Sid running off with your mom. All the stuff I'm not supposed to know about."

"Oh," was all I could think of to say. This was a lot to take in after weeks stuck in Alcatraz, playing blind, deaf, and mute. A hell of a lot.

Danny said, "Look, I gotta motor. I'm writing down directions for you to take the subway. You can call me from a pay phone if you get lost. It would be crazy to drive down with the traffic and parking in this city." I liked that he trusted me enough and thought I was smart enough to take the subway by myself in a new and strange city.

Still, I wanted to say, forget about directions, could you just stop your life for the rest of today and sit down and tell me all this business about Sid-dad and Frank-dad, like in painful and excruciating detail? But Danny was already slinging his carry bag over his shoulder and looking at his watch like he was running late, and anyway, I felt a little weird about begging for a heart-to-heart when we'd only just met.

Then just in time I figured out a way to get to know Danny better. "I am a barista, you know," I said as he opened the door to leave. "If you need help. I used to have a job until my parents made me quit. I make killer coffee."

Danny said, "Cyd Charisse, you've got yourself a deal. Come around today at three and we'll give you an apron and put you to work."

He kissed me on the cheek and walked out. He waved behind his back to me and yelled out, "See you later, charm girl," as he walked down the generic hallway to the elevator.

I don't need a driver to figure this all out. I'm doing pretty damn good on my own.

Twenty-three

I was too busy being psyched about new barista gig and my new most adorable older brother to think about Blank. Then Luis came by and he was so honeylicious that my heart couldn't help but go south with longing for a cute boy to be all mine to snuggle up with, even in this sticky humid New York weather.

"So you gotta plan for what you wanna do today?" Luis asked.

Concentrating on what Luis says is difficult, he is so FINE to look at.

"Huh?" I said back. Because really I was, once again, inspecting his bulging biceps and wondering about his sure-to-be six-pack abs. "Do you work out?" I couldn't help myself asking. Concentrate, Cyd Charisse, I told myself. Think about cotton ball sky clouds, think about old locker combinations, do NOT think about that bod. Trouble.

Luis said, "Yup. Every morning I'm at the gym six sharp. Used to wanna be a boxer. Got too many injuries, though. So now I'm taking college courses in business and working for your da . . . ," pause, "your unc . . . ," pause, "your . . . Frank part-time, driving and running errands and stuff."

"How do you know 'my Frank'?"

"His family's former housekeeper is my aunt."

"Miss Loretta."

"Right! How'd you know that?"

"I hear she makes the best gingerbread ever." Gingerbread and I shared a telepathic moment. She knew we have a date with destiny with Miss Loretta, who in some ways is Gingerbread's spiritual mother, if you think about it.

"You're right about that. So whadya say, want to go explore big bad New Yawk?"

"I have a job," I said. "Starting this afternoon."

"Do you now? Where is it, I'll drive you there. Frank said I should take you where you want to go."

I don't need a twelve-step program to figure out where I need to go without a driver. I said, "Thanks, but I'll take the subway."

"Frank know about this?"

"I can take care of myself," I said, and I think I believed it. Besides, after talking with Danny, I didn't want Luis driving me around if that whole deal was really about Frank-dad trying to be competitive with Sid-dad. I wanted no part of it, even if it meant an opportunity to cozy up to Luis.

Luis shrugged. "I got the car in the garage for now. You insist on taking the subway, I'm taking the subway with. No way some sixteen-year-old girl never taken the subway before is going on the subway by herself. You hungry? Let's go grabba slice."

"Grabba slice? What does that mean?" I supposed I wouldn't mind—at all—hanging out with gorgeous Luis, so long as he wasn't driving me. A generous sacrifice on my part, I know. On the babe scale, Luis was like an NBA-sized Blank. How much would I have liked to just spend the afternoon on the sofa making out with him and just fuggedabout driving and subways and everything else? Mucho.

"Pizza, doofus," Luis said, pretend shoving me. He spoke slowly for him in what probably would have been normal pace for someone like from Idaho or something, "Go . . . grab . . . a . . . slice . . . of . . . pizza."

"Do you have a girlfriend?" I asked Luis as we headed toward the elevator. I know, it's like a disease I have, cute boys.

"Why? You got a friend who wants to put in an application?" Luis winked at me.

"Maybe," I said. "How old are you?"

"Just turned twenty," he said. "You got any girlfriends old enough for me?"

I guessed that was Luis's nice way of telling me I was jailbait.

"I don't have friends my age," I told Luis.

"No boyfriend back in Frisco?" he asked.

"Nobody calls it Frisco. People call it The City. It's like this stupid rule people obey."

Luis repeated, "No boyfriend back in Frisco?"

"I had a true love but he dumped me," I said. I sighed. The elevator stopped for us and we stepped in.

"His loss," Luis said. "Beautiful girl like you. He'll wake up. Trust me."

I hit the STOP button on the elevator as it was going down. The elevator came to a sudden halt. "Do you really think so? Because I am getting kind of worried."

Luis hit the START button and the elevator proceeded back down. "If you're meant to be together, you'll figure it out. You must have lots of other friends to hang out with, right? While you and your ex figure things out?"

"No," I told Luis as we arrived at ground level. "I am the girl at school that even the weird kids think is too weird."

"That just means you're the coolest girl in school," Luis said.

"Thank you, Loo-eese," I said. I pretend shoved him back as we walked out into the hot sticky summer to go grabba slice.

Twenty-four

So I might be totally lost in this vast and strange new freakcity, but there's one gig where I totally know the scene, and that is making coffee. Pressing beans, steaming milk, pouring perfection: Here at the Village Idiots, Danny and Aaron's café, I have a little pocket of belonging in this city of millions.

"Wow," Danny said, "you were really trained well. I don't have to teach you anything except where the supplies are."

"You are a godsend!" Aaron, Danny's boyfriend, said. "I didn't know how we were going to survive the rest of the summer without a decent barista. The only people we can afford to pay are out-of-work actors, and they are too busy looking into the mirrors to make decent coffee. Cyd Charisse, where have you been all our lives?"

Funny question, huh? That's what I thought about them. Their café was quite possibly cooler than Java the Hut at Ocean Beach. The café was decorated with medieval wall hangings and gothic wood chairs and had gilded mirrors on the ceilings which reflected back the most sumptuous joy you could imagine: Danny's cakes. Some were soft and delicate, light chocolates with mousse petals, others were towering layers of buttermilk heaved with iced rose bouquets. Each cake was its own artistic masterwork. Not that the beauty of them prevented me from random samplings of as many as I could stomach. Hello Delicious, my new friend.

In the back room, Danny showed me a few of his special-order naughty cakes which he makes for "bachelor" parties in the West Village and Chelsea. The cakes were not vulgar or crude. They were anatomically correct visions of beauty. Danny sure knew how to put pink icing, chocolate sprinkles, and whipped cream to good effect. I must confess, some of the cakes made me kind of hot. It was a good thing Loo-eese said his good-bye, after taking me on the noisy-crammed-manic-cool subway train and letting me cop a feel on his thundering biceps when I saw huge rats scurrying across the tracks.

Catch my breath.

Even better than Danny's cakes and Aaron's mega-delish pasta salads and quiches was the knowledge that, at least for my parole in Manhattan, I would be properly caffeinated. The Village Idiots favored Italian coffee over Java the Hut's Indonesian, but I attributed the diff to an East Coast/West Coast thang and decided I could be hip to the new coffee groove. The taste was totally different but the coffee outtasite. Energy returned to Cyd Charisse.

"Va-va-va-voom, Cyd Charisse!" Aaron proclaimed after I gulped my first straight double espresso shot and shouted out "HIIIIIIIIIII-YAAAAHHHH" like a banshee and then shimmied with caffeinated pleasure. Gingerbread, who was reclining in a giant porcelain coffee mug, rolled her eyes at me. I know, I know, I telepathed back, I don't have to try so hard, he's just a long-lost brand-new brother, but it's just all so good and where do I feel more at home than at a coffee-house surrounded by gorgeous guys? Just deal, okay?

I liked Aaron, and not in a dangerous Java-my-heart-beat-races-when-he's-within-five-feet-of-me radar kind of way. Aaron was not pretty-boy cute, or smoldering like Java. He was tall and chunky and scruffy, and for an upstanding homosexual, not that great a dresser, what with his faded decal Aerosmith T-shirt and his worn-out pajama pants he wore because of the oven heat. He was a mellow type of dude with a shock of strawberry red hair creeping out under his tall white chef's hat that he wore even though he cooked for a little café and not a four-star shi-shi restaurant, and he had big baby blue eyes that softened every time he looked at Danny. How could you not like him?

Danny and Aaron met at boarding school. They have been together that long, like almost ten whole years. High school sweethearts. They gave me hope.

Sid and Nancy have been together for just a little bit longer, but you would never see them sharing a business together, or not freaking that the business doesn't make a ton of money—hardly any actually—or bring them lots of influence and admirers. You would never see one of them bring the other ice wrapped in a washcloth when the other burned a finger and then kissing the finger to make it better, you would never see them laughing over old jokes and having hearts open enough to allow a new sister into their lives without feeling threatened or put out.

Danny wanted to take the evening shift off to spend time with me and Aaron was all, "Cool, go, have fun." One time Blank and Java didn't come to work because their cousin was visiting, and I counted the minutes until my shift ended that day, I was so uptight about them having fun without me and forgetting about me. I broke three glasses that day and sulked when Blank asked me how my day was on the phone that night. Ouch.

I was grateful that Aaron was a lot sweller about sharing Danny than I would have been about Blank. I had only known my brother for a day, and I wanted to spend as much time with him as he would give me. I wanted to suck information from him like a sponge. And anyway, when Danny called Frank-dad to tell him he was kidnapping me for the night, I swear I could hear the sigh of relief coming from Frank's end of the phone, even though Danny said "daddy" was annoyed with him for making my acquaintance without consulting Frank first. I had a feeling that's how things were done in his biological corner of the family: Everyone just did what they wanted and then told Frank, because you couldn't rely on him to take care of things the right way.

"So tell me about yourself, charm girl whom I'm going to call CC," Danny said when we finally sat down to dinner at about eleven that night. We had planned on ditching the Village Idiots much earlier, but the café got so busy, and I was churning out the lattes so smooth and Danny was dishing out the cakes so fine, that we ended up just staying a couple extra hours because Ella blasting from the stereo sounded so good and the all-over vibe, with customers chattering, forks clinking, coffee slurping, people happy, we just couldn't desert Aaron until after the crowds left, they tummies full, they teeth tingling.

"No," I said. "You first." I wanted to bask. We were seated at an outdoor café, which you can never do in San Francisco because it is too cold at night; it felt great to sit outside at night wearing only a black tank dress and combat boots and not be freezing. I liked Greenwich Village much more than Frank Land on the Upper East Side. There were no skyscraper office buildings or condo complexes, but loads of old brownstones, funky restaurants, and little parks where people played rapid-fire dominoes and chess with timers set on the sides of the tables.

Being the little sister, even though Danny is about my same height, being looked after and cherished, was even better. I hope one day when Ash and Josh are grown up we can come back to the Village and have dinner and bond. Hopefully Sid and Nancy will keep it together and we won't have to spend our sib time talking about our parents' secrets and lies, the way Danny and I were going to have to spend our first dinner.

Twenty-five

"So this is how it went down," Danny explained. "I was barely in middle school at the time, and so I've had to put together the pieces over the years, and my facts are not one-hundred percent reliable, but here's what I know. Daddy and your mom were having an affair and then she got pregnant. I'm sure they talked about having an abortion—if I'm making you uncomfortable just tell me—but she decided to have the baby. I think she expected Daddy to marry her, and I think Daddy wanted to. My parents' marriage was awful, you should know that. My mother spent most of her time at our house in Connecticut, and Daddy had an apartment in the city where he spent weeknights. Really, we only saw him on weekends when I was a kid. He was a workaholic and was, and still is, a womanizer. This is fact. CC, I can tell by looking at you and talking to you that you're not so innocent and naïve that you can't hear this stuff—I think you get it and I think you can understand that our father can still be a loving father even though as a husband or lover, he was no angel. Right?" Danny looked a little worried that he had said too much too soon.

I nodded. I was sad to hear Danny proclaim what I already suspected to be true, but at the same time, I think I felt a little relieved not to have to put Frank real-dad up on any pedestal anymore. Also, I liked Danny for laying down the facts without sugar-coating, much as I love sugar.

"My mother would not give him a divorce. She was a

very devout and serious Catholic, and I think she wanted to spite him, too. She held him responsible for all of her unhappiness."

"Did you hate your mom?" I asked Danny. Because even though Nancy and I aren't exactly going to be cat-walking at any mother-daughter fashion shows anytime soon, I don't hate her at all, despite what she thinks. She makes me crazy and I think she totally does not get me, but I know that in her mind, she tries to do what is right for me, even though what she thinks is right usually results in decisions I hate, i.e., boarding school, puke princess room, Alcatraz incarceration. I realized it must have been a huge leap of faith for her to let me come to New York on my own and find out things that I might not like. I wondered if, in her own way, maybe she was trying to allow me an independence that would nudge my grow-ing up process along.

"No," Danny said, "I loved my mother very much, even though she thought my being gay was a sin. She was very controlling, but she loved us and would have done anything for us. My sister is a lot like her."

"Do you miss her?"

"I do miss my mother," Danny said. "We fought a lot when I was a teenager. She didn't approve of Aaron and was always referring to him as my 'friend.' She never told her friends I was gay. But at the end of her life, when the can-cer was eating her away, I spent a lot of time with her, nurs-ing her, talking to her. Aaron did, too, and that made a huge difference. She finally got to know him and see how won-derful he was and appreciate him as my lover and my mate. The denial wore away, and I think she came to love him as much as she could. He was very good to her, especially considering that initially she had been awful to him."

"What about my dad?" I asked.

"Daddy has always been great about Aaron, but in a very stiff way . . ." When I asked about my dad, I had meant Sid-dad. Sid-dad who had always been there for me, who loved me as much as he loved Ash and Josh, who would never try to pass me off as his niece. "It's like he was trying so hard to be cool about the whole situation that eventually he just came to accept it."

"What about 'Uncle' Sid?" I clarified.

Now Danny smiled. "I miss him!" he said. "When I was little, he was like a hero to Lisbeth and me. He didn't have a wife or children so when he came to visit, he would take us to amusement parks and baseball games. He had an inexhaustible supply of energy for us. You could tell he wanted kids but he was also a workaholic and he didn't date much. And then Daddy made the mistake of asking his old pal Sid to watch over his girlfriend and love child in the city one weekend and it was all over after that. Uncle Sid, I guess, was so furious at Daddy about the way Daddy had behaved—leading double lives and lying to my mom and to your mom—that he stopped talking to Daddy, and soon after that, I guess your mom realized he was never going to marry her or help her raise their child, and she broke things off with Daddy. And then like a year or two later, Sid came back into town, got in touch with your mom, fell in love with you from the way I understand it, and whisked you both away to San Francisco, which worked out very conveniently for Daddy and my mom because the whole situation had become this silent onus that everyone knew about but nobody talked about, it made them total enemies. Lisbeth and I were trapped in the middle of a very unhappy family."

More score: For all that, in my opinion, Danny had a lot to be bitter about, he accepted everyone in his family for who they were, warts and all, and seemed to love them each individually just the same. I was starting to feel like my older baker brother was a helluva good inspiration, maybe even better than Helen Keller, should I choose to heed his enlightened call.

"Okay, Ceece, now it's your turn. Spill. Tell me about you."

For once I think I felt shy and I kind of rolled my eyes and shrugged and turned the corners of my mouth down. "Dunno!" I said.

"Boyfriend?" Danny asked. "Girlfriend?"

"Well," I said. "I had like a true love in San Francisco. He is an artist and a surfer and a barista, too." As I was talking, my skin was actually tingling from missing He Who Cannot Be Named.

"And?" Danny asked.

"My mother made me not see him anymore and then he dumped me."

Danny eyed me and said, "Something tells me there's more to the story than that."

"Well, I spent the night at his house and then my parents grounded me and then he decided that I was harshing his mellow and he needed some time to, like, do things with other people and do his art blah blah blah."

"Hmm," Danny said. "Aaron and I had a period like that, right after high school. We broke up for like six months because we thought we wanted to see other people, thought we needed to experience more things separately, independently."

"But you worked it out!" I said excitedly. "You decided it's better to be together!"

"We did. But the time apart was good. We did need to work on our own individual identities. We still do."

"Oh," I said. "Right."

"Do you have lots of friends? You don't seem like one of those squealing teenyboppers who travel in packs and like to scream for pop stars in Times Square."

"My best friend is Sugar Pie. She lives in a nursing home. She is a psychic and can read tarot cards."

"Interesting! Do you get along with your mom?" Danny asked.

I hesitated, then said, "We try." I could try to try, I considered.

"Do you have plans for your future? Do you know what you want to do?"

I shook my head. "I don't understand those people who have it all figured out, who know 'I want to go to XYZ College and then I'll be a lawyer' or a weatherperson or whatever. I'll be lucky to get into junior college. Anyway, maybe I just want to be a barista."

"You could do worse," Danny said. "You're great at that, and the most important first steps in figuring out what you want to do, you already have—a good work ethic and loving what you do."

Hmm.

I yawned and looked at my watch. It was past one in the morning, and the streets were still teeming with people and life, laughter and music. I was drained, not just sleepy tired, but emotionally exhausted.

"Are you tired?" Danny asked. "Maybe you want to just crash at our place tonight rather than go back uptown to Daddy's?"

I surprised myself when I said no. It was almost like we had sprinted to the finish line of our sibling learning curve, and now we needed a breather, because we had cheated past years of growing, struggling, fighting, and adoring to get to this one day and night of perfect togetherness. "I'll take a cab back to Frank's," I said.

I looked up at the Empire State Building. I had been born at a hospital on the East River in the shadow of this monolith. Pieces of the jigsaw puzzle that is Cyd Charisse started to feel like they were being identified and put in their proper place.

Twenty-six

After five days of me grabbing a slice with Luis at lunch and then working the dinner shift at the Village Idiots, Frank has decided that I am worthy of his time. He has done me the immense favor of clearing his social calendar on Saturday until five o'clock, after which he has to get dressed and leave for the theah-tah. We are going to be father-daughter until the clock strikes five and I am flying solo and Frank is off wining and dining clients and hopefully not impregnating impressionable young dancer-models.

We started with a walk through Central Park. For once the weather was not that sticky and the sun beamed down through the midtown skyscrapers onto the lush greens of the park as we strolled, not walking close like chums, but at a slight distance from each other as, I suppose, wayward dads and their love children are wont to do.

Frank was very proud of himself when we arrived at Strawberry Fields on the West Side.

"See," he said. "This area was dedicated to John Lennon, who lived right over there." He pointed to a haunted-looking old apartment building creeping over the trees in the distance.

"Who's John Lennon?" I asked, and Frank's face fell.

"He was a musician and a songwriter and a revolutionary. People come from all over the world to see this tribute to him." How much do you want to bet he gleaned this information from a commercial? I offered a blank stare back and Frank added, "Ever hear of the Beatles?"

"I think so," I said, but I was humming a song to myself: Yeah yeah yeah. Torturing Frank on the generation gap like this was somewhat amusing.

"Many people thought John Lennon was a hero," Frank said very seriously. "Your brother Danny worshiped him." You could tell Frank was real pleased with himself for knowing about this spot with the oval that proclaimed "Imagine."

"Oh, I remember," I said. "Wasn't he also the guy that was like doped up all the time and having an affair with some other Asian lady that wasn't his wife?"

Frank looked down and then back at me. "You're not going to make this easy for me, are you?" he asked.

"Nope," I answered, but in a very pleasant way.

We walked in silence for a while. As we approached the middle of the park, Frank said, "Are you interested in art? We could walk over to the Metropolitan Museum from here."

"I like art," I said. "I especially like artists."

Frank gave me a quizzical look back. We changed directions and started heading back to the East Side. We stopped for crushed lemon ices from a rolling cart vendor, and as we proceeded with our stroll, sour-sweet lemon quenching our thirst, Frank kind of cleared his throat and then said to the open air in general and not directly at me, "So, are you . . . uh . . . managing to stay out of trouble?"

I realized that in his way Frank was trying to make sure I was okay and part of me suspected that was probably the best I would ever get out of him. "Yup," I said. "I'm on the pill now."

Frank blushed, which was funny considering all the women with spaghetti-strap sundresses and bloodred-painted toenails whom he had been covertly eyeing all afternoon. And even with his East Coast docksiders on his feet and his goofy polo shirt and khaki shorts and his sixty-something self, they had been scoping him back. Blech!

Maybe Frank has produced too many public service announcements as the King of the Advertising World because he said, "Your boyfriend and you . . . you practice . . . you be sure to be safe. The pill is not enough."

"I know," I said. It's funny that I would not want to have this conversation with Nancy, but since Frank is a certified dawg, it did not bother me at all. "Condoms are good, too." I gave him a friendly punch in the arm and said, "You remember that, old buddy!"

Frank did laugh. I think he realized that there was just too much awkwardness between us so why not just suspend it entirely?

Frank relaxed and said very bluntly, "This boyfriend of yours. He was the one that got you into trouble?"

"Nope," I answered. "That was the boyfriend before." I could tell Frank was a little relieved that he wasn't going to have to give me a speech about continuing in a relationship with a boy who knocked me up and then stuck me with looking up my secret father to wire me the money to pay for the abortion. "I'm actually not seeing anybody right now. My boyfriend in San Fran broke up with me." Now Frank looked double relieved. Not only did he not have to give me the aforementioned speech, but he also did not have to worry about me fooling around with a current boyfriend. And yet he was the one that threw Luis into my hormonally challenged world! Irony.

Having dispensed with the safe-sex talk, Frank was free to move on to tamer topics. "So, do you have a favorite subject in school?"

"Skipping school is probably my favorite subject. I just cannot get myself interested in anything that goes on there."

"Don't you want to go to college?"

"Eh," I shrugged. I know it's super cool to be one of those hyper-achieving teens who kill themselves on extracurriculars and cram for SATs and write extra credit reports about saving the environment to get higher GPAs, but I am just not one of those people. I may, in fact, be one of those people who will be content just to make great coffee and hang out on foggy broody beaches and not worry too much about the great issues of the world. I don't think that makes me a bad person.

"Your sister," Frank said proudly, "was a stellar student. Went to Harvard, my alma mater. She's now an investment banker with a top Wall Street firm."

"When am I going to meet this sister?" I asked. Rhonda lisBETH was like the dark shadow of my visit so far. Everyone seemed to dance around the issue of her, like she was some kind of monster who couldn't be unleashed upon love children.

"Soon," Frank said, although I don't think he believed that. Clearly, lisBETH was the person who did not want to meet me.

We arrived at the grand steps of the Met where swarms of people were milling about, sitting around and drinking sodas, taking pictures, chilling in the hot summer breeze. "So what'll it be," Frank asked as we walked up the steps. "Egyptian artifacts, Asian pottery, Renaissance paintings, what's your pleasure?"

I said, "I don't like that portraits of ancient kings and queens and velvet tapestry stuff. I dig on more modern kinda art. Not that streaks of paint splashed across a canvas that a four-year-old could do, but like that cube stuff and Picasso-ness and that guy who drew windows and that lady who did the erotic flowers and oh, I especially like that guy who did the intricate mathematical-like black-and-white pictures of like hands and buildings and such."

Frank looked impressed, actually. I have no idea why. "You mean you like Magritte and Georgia O'Keefe and Escher?"

"Yeah!" I exclaimed. "Those guys!" Shrimp used to love dragging me to museums on the days we skipped school together.

"Hmmph," Frank said, pleased.

While we were standing in the admission line, some old white guy wearing golf pants and a shirt with a little alligator came up to us. "Frankie!" the guy exclaimed. "Good to see you, good to see you. What brings you to the Met in the middle of summer when most respectable people are on the Vineyard or in the Hamptons? Heh heh heh." I locked my eyes into place to prevent them from rolling in disgust. I hate snobs.

Frank gestured toward me and said, "I'm showing my nie . . ." He looked at me and I bore my eyes straight to the center of his soul, and he continued, "my . . . my . . . my goddaughter, showing her a little bit of the city. She's a modern art fan! Quite knowledgeable, too."

Oh, please. I know Frank wanted me to give an innocent and sweet smile to his friend but I didn't. I just stared ahead blankly.

You could tell the old guy was confused and had probably never before seen a goddaughter that looked exactly like her godfather, but if he suspected anything, he didn't let on. The old guy gave me a friendly tap on the shoulder. "Well, enjoy! See ya later, old fellow. Lunch at the club soon?"

Frank said, "Definitely. I'll have Dolores call your girl."

"Excellent, will do," the old guy said, and proceeded back toward his own family.

When he was gone, Frank cleared his throat again and said, "That was the CEO of one of my biggest clients."

I suppose "goddaughter" was the best compromise he could give. I wasn't even mad. I wasn't. That's just Frank, I guess.

He must have mistook my silence for my wanting an explanation because he added, "CEO. That's the Chief Executive Officer. It's the head guy for an important company."

"I know what one is, Frank," I said. "My dad is one."

We both knew I meant Sid-dad, my real dad.

Twenty-seven

So in the Biological Father of the Year category, Frank might not be winning any awards anytime soon. He asked if I would like Luis to hang out with me on a Saturday night. Would I! Nancy would have choked on her LifeSavers before allowing a Luis-like hottie to "baby-sit" me for a Saturday evening, but Frank didn't think twice about it.

I was good, though. I said no. Frank didn't expect to be home until very late and he seemed like he almost felt bad about leaving me alone. Danny and Aaron had invited me to par-tay with them in the Village, but they had spent all their evenings of the last week working with me and laughing with me, so I figured they needed a night for just them without Cyd Charisse, third wheel. God only knows where Rhonda lisBETH was, not like I cared anymore.

I knew that the warm and sultry summer air was beckoning Temptation just too strongly, so I said, don't you worry about me, Frank. I don't need Luis to chaperone me. I'm gonna watch this here satellite TV and order me some moo shoo something or other and we'll be just fine. Gingerbread and I will hang out and hit the sack early, *no problemo*. I meant it when I said it, too, and Frank was all, Well, Luis said to call him if you want company, and I said, Right.

So even though TV usually bores me, I got sucked in by this cheesy '80s movie about this dorky pizza delivery boy who mistakenly becomes this gigolo to all these posh women. And the thing about the pizza delivery boy was that he was kinda skinny and scrawny and average-looking, but he was all heart, and somehow, he managed to turn himself into what each of the women's fantasies were.

This, of course, made me think of Blank, because of (a) the pizza boy's good heart, (b) he was a great loverboy, and (c) did I mention the warm and sultry summer weather that just seduces your skin?

But still, I was good. Gingerbread gave me a look like, Don't do what I know you're thinking about doing, by which she meant, Don't be fooling with my boy Loo-eese. I told her, Don't you worry, it's cool.

I had another plan in mind. A call-by. A call-by is what I call the telephone equivalent of a drive-by, when you're crushing on someone so you figure out a way to drive by their house to see if they're home, if the lights are on, if, oh my goodness you're hanging out on the porch and I just "happened" to be driving by, why don't we go out for coffee or something? Coincidence! Call-by's usually end, however, when you listen to the object of your affection saying, "Hello? Hello? Who is this? Goddamnit, who is this?" and you sigh because you love that person so much and then you hang up. Call-by's, by the way, are not advisable if the person on the receiving end has Caller ID, which I knew for a fact that the recipient of my call-by did not have, or if that person is a chronic *69er (which is an interesting numeric choice on the part of the phone company, in my opinion).

So I picked up that phone and Gingerbread closed her eyes, and the phone went *ring ring* and my heart went flutter flutter. After six rings I was about to hang up when a voice answered very sharply, "Ya, what?" Java. My lust factor shot through the ceiling even though I wanted to ask him, How is you-know-who? Is he okay? Does he miss me like I miss him? Have you fired that incompetent piece of shit Autumn yet?

But my mouth froze and my body grew warm and almost instantly, there was a fire inside me that was going to need to be quenched. I could almost hear the roar of the Ocean Beach surf in the distance and see Java standing in his wet suit on the roof, the cordless at his ear as he stared longingly at the water, hungering for the cold curls.

To the silence, Java said, "Who's there? Hello? Delia, is that you? Listen baby, you know I'm sorry about last night . . ."

I hung up.

I remembered how Blank's last words to me had been, "And maybe you need some time to figure out your crush on my brother." I looked at my Mickey watch. Seemed to me like that time had come. I looked at Gingerbread and she was giving me that same look she used to give me before I would sneak off to Justin's room to fool around. I took Gingerbread into our bedroom and tucked her in for the night. I whispered in her ear, "Don't worry, I'll be careful." I gave her an eskimo kiss and placed my sleep mask over her eyes so the moonlight would not keep her awake or distracted.

I returned to the living room and called Luis's mobile phone.

"Hey, buddy," I said in this indifferent but kind of sexy way.

"Uh-oh," Luis said. "What, you don't like being home alone on a Saturday night?"

"Maybe," I said, coy. "Maybe not."

This is how I used to be around Justin. And he actually fell for this, too. Men. I don't get them.

Luis said, "So what do you want me to do about it?" I could hear laughter and music in the background of wherever he was.

I said, "I was thinking of going out clubbing tonight. Got any recommendations for places to go?"

Luis said, "No, you're not! Frank'll kill me!" I think he covered his hand over the phone because there was a pause and what sounded like a voice softly exclaiming, "Fuck!" Then he came back to the phone and said, "What do you say I come over and you and me go get a coffee or some tea?"

"Long Island Iced Tea?" I asked.

Luis said, "NO! I'll be over soon. Man, girl, I took one look at you and knew you were trouble." The tone of his voice was not entirely displeased by that observation. "Don't go anywhere, I'll be over soon."

"'Kay," I said, and hung up.

Her natural psychic abilities must be greater than Sugar Pie's because guess who called exactly when I hung up with Luis? My mother. How does she know when I'm about to score?

"Oh, hi," I said, nervous. Since arriving in New York I had talked to Nancy once, when I was in the car on my way to Frank's from the airport and I had called to tell her I arrived okay. She had promised then she wouldn't call me every two minutes and she had been pretty good about it. She had promised we would give each other "space."

"How are things going, sweetie?" she asked. "Is your

da . . . is he . . . is Frank there?" I don't know what is wrong with people. Nobody knows how to address what Frank and I are.

"No, he went out," I said.

Nancy sighed, of course. "Surprise surprise," she said. "What are you doing now? Are you home alone?"

"Gingerbread and I are watching TV," I said.

Nancy sighed again. "Don't you think it's time for you to give up that doll?"

Silence.

"No."

"Did I hear you say you're watching TV?"

Silence.

"Yes."

I could hear Ash and Josh in the background screaming and knocking things around.

"I can't hear anything!" Nancy shouted to them.

"I wasn't saying anything," I told her. "You didn't miss anything."

"Well," Nancy said sternly. "We miss you here. You stay out of trouble and if you need anything, call me."

I suppose she was trying to be nice but all I could think about was how she grounded me so I couldn't see the love of my life and how she was responsible for him dumping me. Who was she to tell me to stay out of trouble? She was my trouble.

"Yeah, right," I said. "Say hi to dad and the kids."

"Love you . . . ," she started to say into the phone but I hung up.

So now I was fired up by Java's voice and pissed off by Nancy. I took a shower to try to cool off. No dice. And who should swim right into my trouble brew but Loo-eese, arriving all glassy-eyed and somewhat tipsy.

"You're stoned," I told him as he walked in.

He didn't respond to my proclamation but handed me a package of Twizzlers red licorice. "Hungry?" he asked.

"Way," I answered. I could feel my wet hair cascading down the bare part of my back, snaking drops of water down my spine, making me shiver with warmth and excitement.

Luis plopped down on the sofa and said, "So, what's really on your mind?"

I am a get-to-the-point kind of girl so I told him, "I know you have been checking me out since I came here and I have been checking you out too and I think we should do something about it."

Luis looked sad and said, "Can't. You're too young. You're Frank's . . . you're Frank's . . . whatever."

"Do whatevers do this?" I put his hand on my hip and leaned in toward him.

Please let me live my Wallace fantasy out on you, I thought, *please help me get it out of my system.*

"Brazen" was the word the headmaster at boarding school used to describe me.

I straddled Luis on the sofa and kissed his neck. "Please, Luis," I whispered into his ear. "Do me this favor. We don't have to go all the way. I don't want you to like have to go to church and say a million Hail Marys because you had consensual sex with an underage girl. But bases one, two, and three are wide open, so why not take a shot at bat?"

Oh, it felt so nice to kiss a guy again after Alcatraz. He

did not even pause to consider my proposal, he just pulled me toward him and our lips went right at it. The great thing about making out with someone who is stoned is that it doesn't necessarily have to lead anywhere; neither of us seemed to need it to. It was just all hands and hair and hot breathing, languorous into forever. And let me tell you, those tight biceps and abs felt great to the touch.

I have no idea how long we fooled around, could have been twenty minutes, could have been an hour. The strange part was that for as good as it felt, the whole make-out session made me feel kind of sleazy, too. It was so absent any kind of connection other than lust. I realized the feeling was one I would also experience if I hooked up with Wallace. My longing for Shrimp—say his name loud and proud—increased exponentially the longer I made out with Luis. I wanted kissing of the soul-kissing variety, and not of the sleazy entice-a-stud-over-to-your-place variety.

Not like the sleaze factor stopped me from gettin' a little booty from Loo-eese. Let's be real. My hormones were digging it. But then, as his hands were smoothing over my bare thighs under my short skirt and I was running my fingers through his hair and I was wondering if we shouldn't just go for home base after all because why not we were so close already, what should we hear but a door slam and a female voice exclaim, "Well, I guess the apple doesn't fall far from the tree."

Luis and I jumped up, all tussled and guilty, to stand before our accuser.

"Aw shit," Luis said, zipping up the pants my hands had only seconds before unzipped, and tucking his shirt back in. He took his bag of licorice off the coffee table and said, "I'm outtie." I don't know which scenario was worse for him: appearing stoned and inebriated or fooling around with the family love child. He scrambled toward the door and muttered, "This family," as he walked out to leave me alone with the monster who was my older sister Rhonda lisBETH.

Twenty-eight

If Danny was the shorter, thinner, and happier of Frank, Rhonda lisBETH was surely the Nellie Olson version: beautiful long hair, but pulled back with a preppy headband, framing a face that would be very pretty but for the scowl that looked, from the lines around her eyes and lips, permanently attached to her face. You could tell right away from looking at Rhonda that she only wore clothes she ordered from catalogs of companies in Maine and she was probably never going to meet a love child–sister she liked.

She said, "Cyd Charisse. Do you have a nickname? I can't imagine being called a movie star's name."

"I like my name," I said, then added, "Rhonda."

She demanded, so abruptly I nearly jumped, "Who told you to call me that!"

"Who told you to drop by without calling first?" I answered. I smoothed my hair down and pulled down the ends of my rumpled short skirt, but my heart was racing, as if on attack alert.

"I thought it was about time we met," she said, all huffy.

"Here we are," I said. "We're meeting."

We stood in front of one another staring one another down, like we were preparing for a shootout. I towered over her by a good four inches.

She couldn't stop staring at me. I wondered if my resemblance to Frank tweaked her out. She asked, "Was that Luis? I haven't seen Luis for years but I could swear that was him." When I didn't answer, she said, "Daddy will not be happy."

Like what, I'm supposed to be afraid that Frank will ground me? Mister Love Child–Spawning Indiscretion man? Yeah, right. He'd probably applaud me for scoring. Chip off the old block, eh? Wink wink. Whereas Sid-dad would have given me a lecture about ladylike behavior and making sure I respected any boy I dated, and making sure that said boy appreciated and respected me.

"That was a friend of mine," I said. In hip-hop speak, I added, "Awright?"

Now Rhonda lisBETH was not just mad, she was confused. She answered, in a very slow and clipped manner, "All right," as if she was correcting my English. Then she kind of sized me up and announced, "So, you're Daddy's little indiscretion."

If she hadn't been so completely nasty, I might have felt bad that she probably had a really unhappy childhood and now spent hours in an overpriced shrink's office working on her anger issues.

I asked, "Have you been tested for Tourette's Syndrome?"

"What are you talking about?"

I let Sugar Pie channel my body and I said all sassy, "Girl, don't trash talk to me. I ain't hearin' it."

My so-called sister got a look of deep offense on her face. She said, "Well, I never!"

"That's right, you never," I said.

She headed toward the door. "I'm not going to stand here and be insulted," she said.

"You started it," I reminded her. "Who are you to call me 'Daddy's little indiscretion'?"

Maybe Rhonda lisBETH was embarrassed she had behaved so badly, or maybe she was just that p.o.'d, but she walked out and slammed the door behind her. I opened it back and said, "Better luck next time!" as she proceeded toward the elevator.

Then I cuddled into bed with Gingerbread, who told me everything would be okay and that I should be nicer to unhappy people.

Twenty-nine

Communes are not meant for families, I suspect. That's why they're communes. You can choose your family if you start your own commune. That's the new rule.

My next commune will be in Greenwich Village. We will wear rainbow flags for clothes, and charm bracelets with pictures of Ann-Margret around our ankles. We will only eat Michelangelo-worthy cakes baked by Danny, and we will dance around to punk rock thrasher music, with subways thundering beneath our floors, making us vibrate with pleasure, but not the sleazy kind.

Our commune will be all beautiful men and me. It will be like that Wonder Woman island in reverse, except we won't have superpowers, although we will all look great and be super strong and we will really dig on our collective philosophy, whenever we figure out what that is.

Since I will be the only girl and since all the boys won't be interested in me in that dangerous way, I will stay out of trouble. I will meditate and figure out ways to get along with the outside species of women who like to get bogged down in petty shit and that's why we had to start our own commune, to get away from them. I won't leave the commune until I'm ready, which could be never.

Thirty

So there was something called a lunchtime poll taken at the Village Idiots, and in this poll it was decided that I was the Village Idiot *du jour*. According to the poll, I overreacted about Autumn and I jumped to conclusions about Shrimp's relationship with her. According to the poll, I should have trusted my boyfriend more and been a little more secure with myself before accusing him of cheating on me. According to the poll of customers, who I might add were very happy munching away on their quiches and cakes so they had no reason to bitchslap me, I was the wrong party, not the wronged party.

One thing about being a barista is you can't just be all coy with your mysterious self. Serving and drinking too many straight shots of caffeine will sear right through that. You have to let your coffee-drinking clientele feel your pain, even if it means telling them your love saga over and over and letting them analyze it and take polls about it and such.

I decided not to hold their opinions against the customers by watering down their lattes or serving them whole milk with their cappuccinos when their lean muscley selves had requested skim. I decided to take their opinions under advisement.

After the poll, Danny came up to me and said, "Were you planning on telling me about your and Lisbeth's visit ever? It's been two days."

"Not particularly," I said. How mad was I? A lot. On top of her nasty insinuations was the fact that she was not some cool older chick who would like take me under her wing and divulge important information about men and sex and want to exchange funky clothes and go get pedicures and make puking noises while we looked at the skinny model freaks in the fashion mags as our feet soaked.

It was lucky a lot of steam was coming from the milk I was foaming so my almost-tears did not seem obvious.

Danny said, "Well, I'd like to know your side of it."

"My side! There are no sides here! She was wrong, simple as that. She busted in on me unannounced and then called me 'daddy's little indiscretion' and was not exactly what you would call gracious and welcoming."

"Ouch," Danny said, which was so cute because he had adopted one of my pet expressions and he said it exactly the way I do. "Take a break, Ceece, let's sit down and have a java."

"Coffee," I said. "Let's not use that word 'java.'"

"Why?"

"Let's just not." Somehow in my rendering of the Shrimp saga to Danny, Aaron, and dozens of Village Idiots customers, I forgot to mention that teensy little part about how I had the major hots for Shrimp's brother. My bad.

The lunchtime-poll crowd had left and the café was nearly empty. Danny and I took seats in the big cushion chairs at the front, by the window looking out onto the Greenwich Village scene.

"Lisbeth said you had some guy there with you."

I sipped my iced mocha and summoned an innocent expression to my face. *Me?*

"Ceece?" Danny said.

Danny was just too nice; I couldn't lie to him. I raised my hand like I was in court and said, "Guilty, your honor."

"Who?"

I squirmed. Danny said, "Please don't tell me it was Luis."

I raised my hand again and repeated, "Guilty."

"Cyd Charisse!" Danny said. He tried to feign shock but I think he was impressed, too. I mean come on, Luis is major score gorgeous. "Does Daddy know?"

"Not unless *your* sister told him."

"She's your sister too," Danny said.

"She's not. She's a biological oddity that I choose not to accept as my blood."

And then who should walk into the café but that same biological oddity. She did not see us sitting in the window but ran right up to the counter where Aaron was tossing a salad.

"Aaron!" she squeaked and it was sad, her tone was totally soft and you could tell by the forwardness of her chest and the happy expression on her stern face that she had a thing for her brother's lover. I'll say this for Frank, he breeds complicated people.

Now Danny took on the innocent expression. "Oh, did I forget to mention I asked her to drop by this afternoon for a visit? She had a business meeting not too far from here."

"You," I accused. If it were possible to be annoyed with someone as adorable as Danny, I was, but I admit, I was also curious. My first meeting with Rhonda lisBETH had been disastrous, but if Danny and Aaron could like her as much as they did, there had to be *something* redeemable about her.

Aaron led her over to sit with us. I would guess he and Danny both knew about lisBETH's crush and they were trying to butter her up.

"Oh, hello," she said when she saw me. "I didn't know you'd be here." She gave Aaron a look like, I have to share you with *her?*

"Likewise," I said. I gave Aaron a look like, do you get a major case of the icks from *It* having a crush on you?

Danny said, "Did you ladies know that both of you have a sweet tooth? You both like my chocolate mousse cake best of all the cakes here, and you both like to drink mochas!"

Now lisBETH and I both gave Danny the same look: You're stretching.

"Well, then," Danny said, deflating. "Aaron and I will just go fix some food for all of us. Why don't you ladies sit here and chat while we're in the kitchen?" They scurried off before we could protest.

It sat down opposite me and once again the staring showdown began. She broke it first by asking, "So, was that your boyfriend the other night?"

"Nah," I said. "Just some guy."

She borderline snorted. "'Just some guy'? Nice. Really nice."

I told her, "If you didn't happen to notice, he was way hot."

There was almost a smile on her dour face. "I'll give you that," she admitted.

"I'll say!" I answered. I did not include, and he's

almost of legal drinking age! Howdya like them apples!

LisBETH said, "How many boyfriends have you had?"

"Major or minor ones?"

There was a stunned pause, then, "Hmm," she said. Somehow I had a feeling lisBETH hadn't had many boyfriends in her life and maybe I should shut up about my bounty of booty. "Excuse me a moment, I need to use the ladies." She hopped up from the table and headed toward the bathroom.

Her premium leather briefcase was lying in the window seat. Danny and Aaron were in the back kitchen. I could not resist. Underneath the tablecloth, I slipped my hand onto the briefcase and unlatched it.

Briefcase contents: one electronic organizer; three huge business documents called prospectuses; a disturbingly organized group of faxes, clipped together in sets of descending order by size; a cosmetics bag containing sunscreen, a Chanel lipstick in a ridiculously tasteful pale color, three tampons (the environmentally correct kind), one mini-bottle of hand sterilizer, and no stash of condoms—not even in the zippered compartment (although there was a business card in there that said only "Paulo" and had a telephone number on it . . . hmmm); a cell phone that was actually a funky crystal blue color; a book called *Forgiving Our Fathers: Successful Strategies for Building Healthy and Happy Relationships;* and a book with a cover by someone called Goethe, but when you opened it up, it was actually a Chicken Soup for the Soul book.

One more thing. There was a small framed picture of Frank, lisBETH, and Danny and their mom. Danny was about five in the picture, lisBETH about ten, and the family was gathered around a Christmas tree opening presents. Danny had tousled bed head and was wearing pajamas with feet and lisBETH's hair was pulled back into two tight ponytails with ribbons and she was wearing a girlie Christmas-colored frock. What kid takes time to get dressed and put their hair into neat ponytails on Christmas morning when there are presents to rip apart? The Rhonda lisBETH kind, I guess. Their mom, who was more homely than pretty, and sort of full-bodied in that unhappy Betty Crocker kind of way, was gazing adoringly at Frank, who was handsomely staring off into the distance, oblivious to the family moment.

So that was the family torn apart by Frank's deceit. I wondered if Nancy had ever seen pictures of Frank's kids when she and Frank were carrying on.

I looked up and saw lisBETH huddled in conversation with Danny at the back of the café. They were all hushed whispers and hand gestures. It looked like Danny was pleading, "Please!"

LisBETH returned to the table, sat down, and announced, "Let's try this over again." She said it more like a demand than a request. "Shall we get together sometime, just the two of us?"

"I'm around."

She said, "I'm at the office most days until about ten in the evening. In fact, I need to go back now for another meeting. How about this Saturday? I think I could fit you in sometime around lunchtime."

"*Could* you?" I said, but she did not hear the sarcasm.

"I could. I'll pick you up at my father's at noon."

"Lucky me." LisBETH took her electronic organizer out to punch in the date. *Her* father's indeed.

I wondered if she had any curiosity about me, if I went to the ladies if she would try to open my plastic Sailor Moon backpack that I bought in Japantown in San Francisco.

Contents: various lipsticks and powder compacts and my birth control prescription strewn across the bottom; the picture of me (laminated) that Shrimp drew the first day we met at Sugar Pie's; crayon letters and school pictures Josh and Ash sent me when I was at boarding school; a pillow I made for Gingerbread in home ec class; my Walkman with a mix tape that Shrimp made me that I actually listen to a lot because it has the songs from *The Sound of Music* interspersed with all these hardcore punk songs; a menu from Java the Hut; a small cosmetics case containing dental floss, a toothbrush, and toothpaste for use after all meals because I have had a major crush on my dentist since I was eight and I like to hear him rave about my dental hygiene; and in the little zipper compartment, a stash of condoms, and in a small case of no particular distinction, a silver baby rattle I bought at the drugstore the day out I found for sure I was pregnant, that somehow I have never managed to remember to throw out.

Thirty-one

Luis hasn't been by all week so Gingerbread and I decided to take matters into our own hands. So to speak. Luis must be a Caller ID kinda fella because he did not answer when I called him on his mobile. That meant I had to go look for him myself.

Frank was working, not like it would have mattered. After two weeks, we had settled into a pattern of don't ask, don't tell. There was never going to be any Daddy/Princess connection between us, and strange as it may sound, I wasn't so bummed about that. Occasional dinners and carefully plotted blocks of "quality time" were the best Frank had to give; frankly, after two weeks of Frank, that was plenty.

Gingerbread and I grabbed the menu from Miss Loretta's House of Great Eats and headed out on our quest for Luis. The funny thing about Manhattan is that on TV and in movies, everyone seems so gruff and the streets so mean. And it's true, when you are pounding the pavement here, masses of people whoosh right past you and nobody bothers to say "Have a nice day," which they are always saying in California and which I personally find creepy, but in New York, if you actually stop for a moment, at a bus stop or a subway station, a newsstand or the grabba pizza joint, if you actually make eye contact with a person and ask for help, they can't wait to help you! People in New York love talking about New York. Stand at the pizza counter and ask for directions to the Village, and five people who were reading their tabloid newspapers or listening to the talk radio and ignoring everybody will all of a sudden perk up and give opinions about different ways to take the bus or subway, or what directions to give the cab driver so the driver doesn't try to cheat you by mistaking you for a tourist and taking the long way. The guy at the newsstand where I asked for directions to Miss Loretta's, who by now knew me because every day I had bought a pack of gum from him on the way to the Village Idiots, practically wanted to walk me to Miss Loretta's, he was so excited I engaged him in direction conversation. Geez. Talk about a mean city—not.

I walked over to Madison Avenue and started walking up, with Gingerbread perched in my designer handbag that Nancy gave me on my last birthday, a bag that in her book is totally chic and expensive, and in my book is a perfect luxury limo for Gingerbread. It was fun to look in the windows at all the posh designer fashions and haute couture wedding gowns—fun except when you think about how people like Nancy starve themselves to wear those chic threads. About twenty blocks up, the fancy stores stopped and the neighborhood changed— the color of it, the stores, the buildings. Now we were in the 'hood. We turned a corner onto a side street and there it was, Miss Loretta's House of Great Eats, in the ground floor of an ancient beautiful brownstone. It was the kind of building so old and cool you could totally imagine that like two hundred years ago some quirky colonial girl lived there, afraid of being found out she was a witch—if brownstones had been around back in that day. And guess who was sitting out on the brownstone stoop listening to some old school funk radio with his buddies: Loo-eese.

"Hey," I said.

"Hey yourself," he said when he saw me. He stood up and walked down the stairs and over to the street, I guess so his buddies would not hear our convo. "Whatcha doin' here?" He looked embarrassed to see me.

"I have a karmic debt to repay," I said.

"Huh?"

"Two words: I'm sorry."

Luis got a little eensy smile on his gorge face. He said very low, "Yeah, me too. That whole scene was so uncool on so many levels."

"I am so hearing you," I said, also speaking low, like we were spies. "I shouldn't have called you when you were with your dudes when I knew you'd feel obligated to come over and keep me out of trouble 'cuz all I was doing was trying to make trouble with you."

"Yeah," he said, "well, I wasn't no choirboy either." Luis paused, appraising me, but not in the scamming kind of way, more appreciatively and respectfully. "Ya know, I wouldn't have thought you would be the type of girl to come up to this neighborhood just to apologize."

"You might think I am spoiled, Luis, but I am not."

"I'm hearing you now," he said. He full-on smiled now and my heart melted but in a we're-going-to-be-friends way because that sleazy feeling when we're more is just not nice.

"So, ya wanna grabba slice, right?" he asked. "Ya wanna know the best pizza place in the projects up the street, right?"

I said, "I want to meet your aunt, Miss Loretta."

"Smart girl," he said. "C'mon in."

The restaurant was in the ground level space underneath the stoop. It had red gingham curtains hanging on the windows, and pretty lace tablecloths on the small number of tables. For a little nook of a place uptown with not that much room, it was packed with people. I went to the counter where a slender black lady with salt-and-pepper hair was manning the register.

Luis said, "Hey, Aunt L, this is Frank's . . . you know."

Miss L looked me up and down. "You're not kidding!" she said. "It's nice to meet you, Cyd Charisse," she said.

I got a sudden case of shy and I mumbled, "Thank you, you too." From inside the designer handbag, Gingerbread was squirming and kicking. I took Gingerbread out of the bag and said, "This is Gingerbread and she was named after the gingerbread you had made that Frank was carrying one time when I met Frank when I was little."

Miss L did not ask how old was I to be carrying a doll. She extended her hand to Gingerbread's. "Nice to meet you, Gingerbread," she said. "I've never met a namesake of my cooking before. I'm honored."

Gingerbread beamed. She's a sweet little rag doll not used to getting such a reception from anyone other than me.

Miss Loretta said, "I'm knowing your father many years. Known him since we're both children, that's how far back we go." How relieved was I that she dispensed with the niece/goddaughter/whatever business.

I said, "Was he always such a dawg?"

She laughed and said, "Pretty much. It's not funny, I know, but it's the truth. Lord, you are the image of him! That must make your momma crazy!"

I said, "You reap what you sow."

Miss Loretta raised her eyebrow at me. "Well, we all make our choices, and our mistakes. And then we learn and we grow and we move on."

Interesting.

Miss Loretta pointed to an empty shelf over one of the windows. "See that empty space there? My favorite doll from when I was a girl sat there until recently. Her name was Flowers and she was given to me by an aunt from Jamaica. Flowers was as black as night and wore a turban on her head and I swear to you, she knew when I was even thinking about being naughty."

Gingerbread gave me a look like, Hmph.

"One of my baby granddaughters took to Flowers about a year ago, and now Flowers is living with her. So there's an empty space just waiting for the right doll, should you ever feel like you and Gingerbread are ready to move on."

I was a little taken aback but Gingerbread seemed intrigued by the possibility. I said, "I have to head down to the Village to Danny and Aaron's. But we will think about it. Thank you, Miss Loretta."

Miss Loretta took a whole homemade gingerbread out of the bakery case and wrapped it up for me. She said, "You tell my Danny he can make cakes pretty enough to be in pictures, but he'll never make gingerbread as good as mine!" She smiled and Gingerbread and I left, content.

Thirty-two

When I arrived later that afternoon at the Village Idiots after the lunch crowd had left, Danny and Aaron were oblivious to my arrival in the deserted café. They were on the floor making out, the slow, sweet, soul-kissing kind.

Sigh. I remember.

I would like to think that if Shrimp and I had stayed together that ten years down the road we would still be into each other like Danny and Aaron are.

The interesting thing about Danny and Aaron is that they are not greedy about their love; they manage to find pockets of together time at the most unexpected moments. They don't need to be touchy-feely PDA all the time to prove how devoted they are. They just are.

I announced, "Excuse me, but I could be like a robber or something."

They unlocked lips. Aaron rolled off Danny, stood up, and said, "Hey, will you help me set up the bandstand for tonight?"

"Righty-o!" I said. Aaron belongs to this laid-back band called My Dead Gay Son that is made up of all these professional guys, straight and gay, whom they've known since college, who jam together whenever they have the time and inclination, with no particular agenda, musically or otherwise. The band is named after this line from some '80s movie that Danny and Aaron have been obsessed with since high school. The line "I love my dead gay son!" is said by this dad at his football hero son's funeral. The football hero, who is totally a homophobic jerk, is found murdered in a compromising position with another football player. I said that doesn't sound like a very funny movie to me and Danny said, Don't take everything so literally, Cyd Charisse. To Danny and Aaron, the father's line from the movie reminds them of how their own dads reacted about their relationship: sort of overly cool and tolerant, masking a lot of confusion and discomfort. Danny and Aaron are always teasing each other, saying "I love my dead gay son!" and bursting into crocodile tears, and then tearing up laughing.

As Aaron and I sat on our knees putting together the bandstand, my brother/baker/genius man went into the kitchen to crumble a section of Miss Loretta's gingerbread into pieces and sprinkle the crumbs over some of that night's cakes. Aaron said, "He's going to miss you so much when you go back to San Francisco. We have loved having you here."

I didn't have many days left in Manhattan. It felt like I had been here a long, long time. I was actually looking forward to going home, much as I adored Danny and Aaron. I wondered if I had grown and changed during my time here—how could I know if there were no physical signs? I knew that the thought of living in Nancy's House Beautiful did not tweak me so much, that I should probably take Danny's advice and try to make actual friends at school and not have my only female friend be a cool chick in a nursing home, and that Shrimp and I were not finished—not by a long shot. In fact, to my mind, maybe I wanted to figure out a way to start fresh. Maybe that's how I knew I had changed, at least a little. I knew if I wanted to try with

Shrimp again, I wanted to try not as the same person I had been the first time around: needy, always looking over my shoulder, distrustful of a good thing.

I answered Aaron. "Danny's just probably glad I'm not a big bleh like his other sister."

"Lisbeth's not so bad," Aaron defended. "She's just a tough nut to crack."

"You've got the nut part right."

Later that night, when My Dead Gay Son was warbling through an old Otis Redding tune and I was foaming a cappuccino for a customer, I felt Danny's arms reach under my arms to give me a hug from behind. I am not an affectionate type of person but I did close my eyes for a sec to savor the moment as Danny nuzzled his head into my neck and whispered, "I'm so glad you came here, CC." For once, I felt totally at ease in time and space, grateful that I could have a relationship with a guy that was safe and tender, even if he was my brother and I had only known him a couple weeks.

Our moment was interrupted when we looked up to see Frank real-dad standing before us at the espresso machine. Danny did not untangle his octopus arms from around me, he just said, "'Sup, Pops?"

Frank blushed a little, I guess from Danny's and my affection. He hadn't spent any time with the two of us together and so he didn't know that we had grown tight in the shifts we had spent together nearly every day when Frank was at work or off gallivanting with clients or women or whomever, but in general not spending time with me when I had specifically come to get to know him.

"Well, hello," he said, somewhat awkwardly. "I came down to see if I could steal Cyd Charisse away for dinner.

She's spent so much of her time here I've hardly had a chance to see her."

Danny kicked me under the counter so I would not say something rude back, as I was about to. Something about being a hypocrite.

"She'd love to!" Danny shouted over the music.

Now I kicked him under the counter.

I said, "I ate already."

Danny said, "Why don't you two go sit down and I'll bring you some dessert?"

"That will be fine, son," Frank said, and I suppressed a giggle from how formal he was.

Danny brought over a piece of perfect pound cake with the gingerbread sprinkles and whipped cream on top. Just one piece, so Frank and I would have to share, and it was amazing-scrumptious, even sharing. Frank drank from a formal tea set and I took a walk on the wild side: a late-night double shot, fully caffeinated café au lait.

My Dead Gay Son was riffing on jazz standards, so it was easier to hear than when the band had been playing Sex Pistols covers. Frank said, before a sip of herbal tea, "Cyd Charisse, you are a lovely girl. A little, er, spunky, but a lovely girl. I want you to know that. Your mother and Sid did a beautiful job."

"They might contest that observation, Frank. But thanks." It wasn't much from him, but it was something. Actually, it felt really, really, really good to hear him say those words, even if I wasn't going to let him know it, not after he'd called me "spunky."

"You understand why I had to make the choices I did?" he asked.

"Yah," I said, but not too convincingly.

Frank pulled his wallet out and reached into the picture section. Underneath a class photo of lisBETH circa fifth grade, he pulled out a picture of Nancy, her blonde hair pulled back by a ribbon, wearing a hospital gown and holding me the day I was born. Her face was so happy and young and lovely, I almost didn't recognize her. Underneath that picture, he pulled out a small photo of me from kindergarten, the year we moved to San Francisco. My black hair was long even then, with ponytail curls, and my eyelashes thick, black, and curly over my almond eyes. I wasn't smiling, but I never smile for pictures. I remember I was so happy the day that picture was taken because Sid-dad had come to school to flip burgers for the school's Halloween barbecue that afternoon and I had been so proud to have an actual dad to show off at school. I had loved that day.

It was good to know that for all the years I had been wondering about Frank, longing to know him, at least a small piece of his heart had been holding on to me as well. I thought about what Miss Loretta had said about growing up and moving on, learning from mistakes. I asked Frank, "If you had to do it all over again, would you?"

Frank said, "Probably. I loved your mother very much." For Nancy's sake, I was glad he said those words, even though I thought he was paying lip service to the Right Thing to Say to Your Love Child. Nancy had been young and beautiful, he had been older and on the make. Shit happens. I don't think someone like Frank is actually capable of loving another person enough to make sacrifices and tough choices that would make him look bad.

Frank added, "But I was not strong enough to do what

was necessary to allow us to be a family. It took your dad coming along to make the hard choices." I felt a small sliver of appreciation seeping in for Frank's unpretty self-realization.

I told Frank, "Did you ever think of me, like on my birthdays?"

"The day hasn't gone by since you were born that I haven't thought of you," he said. "And when you're ready for college, you'll find a trust fund I set up for you, to which I contributed money every year on your birthday, for your future."

"I don't need money," I said. I hate when adults revert to that topic. It's so ugly. "And for your information, maybe it would have been a lot nicer if you had, like, sent a card or something every year, so that I would have known you were thinking about me."

Frank said, "Your mother and I agreed it would be in your best interest for us to have no contact, to save you the confusion of two fathers, one of whom could not participate in your upbringing."

"Nice of you guys to make these decisions for me."

"You were a child, you couldn't have known what to do. We agreed it was best to wait until you were older, until you wanted the connection, could understand it."

That answer was so lame and unsatisfactory, however true it was. I told Frank, "I don't think I'm planning on going to college. Maybe you could just give the money to Danny and Aaron. They can barely keep this business alive what with the cost of doing business in this neighborhood."

"It's your money to do with as you please, when you are of legal age to assume the trust."

This was not a scene that was going to end in octopus hugs, but I did allow, "What I needed was time, Frank. And I got it, and I'm glad for it. I needed to know you. I don't have to wonder 'what if' anymore. I know."

Frank's head hung low as he absently stirred his tea around. I think he was glad My Dead Gay Son had switched to a Led Zep tune that was deafening the room.

Thirty-three

Rhonda lisBETH arrived for our lunch date exactly at noon, dressed in preppie white shorts that fell just above her knobby knees, a tucked-in forest green polo shirt and white tennis shoes with exactly no scuffs on them and the kind of tennis socks with a little fuzz ball at the back in a coordinated forest green color. Her gorgeous black hair with the strands of gray was tucked under a white golf visor.

Not even a "hello." She looked at me and said, "You're wearing *that?*" Who would have thought lisBETH to be afflicted by a case of Nancyitis?

I looked down at my combat boots, short black skirt, and New York Knicks b-ball sleeveless net jersey, boys size. "What's the prob?" Seemed to me the fashion police should have been descending down on her, not me.

"You don't think that outfit is rather . . . revealing?"

"Only on the lay-up, lisBETH, only on the lay-up." I made a clucking sound with my mouth.

"What's a lay-up?"

I made a dribbling motion with my hands and raised my eyebrows at her, as if to say, does this look familiar? LisBETH's face showed zilch comprehension. "Oh, never mind," I said.

She hustled past me over to the dining table and spread out a garment bag she had been carrying in her arms. She turned to me and announced, like she was a military general, "I brought something for you."

I admit I was curious about the very old-looking garment bag. LisBETH did not seem the crazy night out on the town type.

She unzipped the front of the bag and I half expected her to pull out a hideous prom-type puke princess dress as some kind of see-how-hip-I-am type of gesture, but instead she pulled out a glorious, narrow-cut, vintage silk Chinese gown in a soft lilac color with small ivory and jade embroidered flowers. It was very simple, elegant, and exquisite.

I said, "I don't understand."

LisBETH walked over with the dress and held it up in front of me. "Just as I thought, the right length," she said. She looked up at me—I am about four inches taller than her—and said, "This dress belonged to my . . . to our grandmother, Daddy's mother. Grandma Molly was quite the character. She ran a liquor joint during Prohibition, married five times, cursed like a sailor, and smoked three packs of cigarettes a day. God, she was an incredibly astute businesswoman, though. She made a fortune on the stock market from her divorce settlements. You look a lot like her, you know? Surprised the hell out of me when I first saw you. I think Daddy sees it too—must terrify him! He deserves it, though. That *should* be his cross to bear, that his secret child should be the image of the mother whose shadow he's spent a lifetime trying to come out of."

I was starting to see what Danny and Aaron had meant about lisBETH not always being so bad. I said, "Do you have a picture of her?"

"Not with me. Some time you'll come to my apartment and I'll show you." Maybe in lisBETH's book, I was starting to become not such a despicable character as well. She said, "Grandma Molly was exceptionally tall, like you, and sort of elegant in spite of herself. This was her favorite dress. I've had it cleaned and stored away for years, but you know what? When I feel this dress, I can still smell her Lucky Strike cigarettes! I can practically see her standing here now, in you, a cigarette in one hand and pointing her finger, bossing us around—'Go make me a sherry!' 'Take Mister Poodle for a walk!'—with the other hand." LisBETH let out a little giggle—a feat I wouldn't have thought possible. "Grandma Molly wanted me to have this dress, but let's be honest here, it was never going to fit me, no matter how much I had it taken up or taken out. This dress is meant for a lovely, lithe, tall girl." Dramatic pause. "Like you."

I looked lisBETH squarely in the eyes and said, "Thank you."

She recognized the moment and said, without a single trace of nastiness, "You're welcome. I thought we could go shopping for some shoes for the dress. Sound good?"

"Oh, yes please," I said.

"Cyd Charisse, for all that you come across as a wild child, I must say, you have impeccable manners."

"Ain't that the truth!" I said as we walked out the door together.

"Shall we make our first stop the Gap?" she asked in a hopeful tone in the elevator. When I made a horror movie face, she said, "But I thought all teenagers like to buy their clothes at the Gap!" She probably picked up that piece of information from some guidebook like *How to Mentor Your Illegitimate Teen Sister.*

"Not this one! I am more of a Tar-jay slash thrift store freak kind of gal. But posh shoes, them's I can go for."

"If you say so," she said, and you know what, as we ventured outside together, I would almost say she was having fun. Almost say I was too.

As we walked toward Madison, I asked her, "So lisBETH, any special guy in your life?"

She sighed, pretty impressively I might add. I'd give her sigh an 8.6. She said, "No, all the men I know are either gay, married, complete imbeciles, or have no money."

I said, "Sometimes the ones with no money are the nicest ones of all."

"You can't own an apartment in a desirable neighborhood and raise a family on nice, Cyd Charisse."

"Yes you can, if you want to," I said.

"Oh," she said, laughing, a little bitter, a little amused. "You *are* naïve. I wish I could be that sure of things." She stopped walking and turned to me. "Listen, I dated a boy in college. Nice guy, from a good family, not terribly bright or a go-getter, but we got on fine. When it came time to graduate, he wanted to get married. I wanted to get a job on Wall Street and then go for my MBA. I thought I had all the time in the world. I told him, we're too young, let's wait, let's see other people. That was Daddy telling me what to do! And you know what? That boyfriend, he married someone else, and funny, I had no idea then he would be the last serious boyfriend I would have. Had no idea the pool would dry up so quickly."

Yikes!

I said, "LisBETH, I think if you really wanted to meet someone, you could. There are like personals and dating services."

She said, "You don't understand. If I marry, it has to be to someone who makes as much money, or more, than me. Who has a respectable career. A professional woman who is poised to become a managing director at a major Wall Street firm cannot just date anybody."

"That's your rule," I told her, resuming our walking. "If I were like some cool painter or electrician guy with a heart of gold, I would think twice before asking you out, with an attitude like that."

"Oh, aren't you precious and wise," she said. "Anyway, what does it all matter? I have resigned myself to being single and I have a wonderful career that takes me all over the world, and if I turn thirty-nine and find myself still single and childless, well, there are ways to have a family without having a husband, you know. You of all people would know that."

That's Rhonda lisBETH, I guess: Give with one hand and take away with the other.

Suddenly I connected the dots to her crush on Aaron. I thought, Aaron and his little swimmers better watch out when Rhonda lisBETH's biological clock strikes midnight, because someone is going to be asked to do lisBETH a very, very special favor, one that would keep her future wee'un "all in the family," quite literally.

I shuddered at the thought and said, "Ya know, maybe now is a good time to go to the Gap?" Because fondling identi-clothes in the Gap was surely a good way to bypass lisBETH's detour down Too Weird Street.

This is America, so of course there was a Gap store within blocks. Do you know that creepy feeling of being watched? That's the feeling I was having while lisBETH and

I were going through the racks of capri pants at the front of the store. Then lisBETH sidled up to me and said, "Don't look now but there's a very hunky young guy standing outside the window who can't take his eyes off of you."

Figure on lisBETH to have the word "hunky" in her vocab. Well, of course I had to look!

And how much do I wish I hadn't. Standing on the other side of the windows at the Gap was Justin.

Thirty-four

Once our eyes locked, there was no turning back. Now he wasn't looking through the window at someone he thought might be me. It *was* me. Lucky me.

He came inside. He seemed smaller than I remembered, although he was still beautiful, in that way that young actors are in movies about rebel boys who are on the brink of manhood and are probably going to die tragic, senseless deaths. He had the kind of deep eyes you could get lost in, chiseled cheeks, and full, sensual, extremely kissable lips.

"Wow," he said. "You look great."

What, you mean I look happy, and content, and not all tortured and panicked? I was speechless. When I didn't say anything back, Justin checked out my b-ball shirt and said, "I didn't know you were a Knicks fan."

LisBETH said, "You know each other?" Her voice was very pleased. Not only was Justin gorgeous, he was wearing a lacrosse shirt from like the snootiest prep school in all of Connecticut.

He introduced himself to her. She said, "Oh, I know that name. Your family lives in Greenwich, right?"

Justin smiled in that smug way. "Yeah," he said. "But I'm hanging out at our apartment in the city for the weekend." He turned to me. "How are you? How have you been? Did you ever get the phone messages I left with your housekeeper with the weird Celine Dion accent?"

I mumble-shrugged. "Mmm."

He asked, "What are you doing here?"

There was a petite, pretty girl with long, straight blonde hair held back by a headband who was casting nervous glances at us from the other side of the window. You just knew she was wearing a pleated skirt and cutesy lace-up shoes with ankle socks and probably Love's Baby Soft perfume.

"Is that your girlfriend?" I said, pointing to her.

He didn't answer, which meant yes. He said only, "I've thought about you a lot."

Point score for lisBETH. She must have realized this was an awkward scene with bad history so she discreetly stepped aside to browse the button fly jeans.

There was only one thing I had to say to Justin. "You let me go there all alone."

And worse, I thought, I continued to sleep with you after that. And I probably would have continued to even longer if the headmaster hadn't found us, expelled us, and returned me home, where I would find out about true love, about kindness and good people.

Justin's hollow beautiful eyes looked away, then back at me. "Cyd, when I called you, the thing I wanted to say was . . ." He stopped cold, paused, then said, "I can't believe you're standing here. I thought you moved back to Frisco."

"Nobody calls it Frisco."

"Um, okay . . ."

"What did you want to say?"

He could not look me in the eyes but he did say it. "Sorry," he mumbled.

I swear my heart was palpitating so fast I thought it

would spontaneously zoom out of my throat and land with a giant red splotch onto a pile of precisely folded white cotton ribbed tees.

Maybe he said it, but I wasn't going to congratulate or thank him for his admission that he was the asshole of the century. I just called out to lisBETH, "I'm ready to go," and bless her, she fell right into line, no questions. We left without so much as a good-bye to Justin.

I did flip him the bird behind my back as we walked out the door.

Thirty-five

LisBETH: "Want to talk about it?"

Me: "No."

LisBETH: "What was that all about?"

Me: "Nothing. He's just some guy."

LisBETH: "If you need to talk . . ."

Me: "I'm okay. Thanks."

Thinking, just keep moving, don't think, just walk, don't think.

I was not okay. I begged out of our shopping adventure, saying I was tired from the humidity and wanted a nap.

When I got back to my room at the Real Dad Corporate Suites, I shut the heavy drapes and snuggled into bed with Gingerbread, lying on my side in a crunched position, getting lost in the quiet hum of the air conditioner.

Frank had gone to New Jersey for the day for a golf tournament his company was sponsoring, not like I would have turned to him for fatherly wisdom. LisBETH was great, actually. She didn't pry, she just said, "I'll be at home if you need somebody." I think she almost wanted me to unload on her, to give her something juicy to dwell on, but I just couldn't. I didn't even call Danny. I guess there is such a thing as getting to know your biological family and making connections with them, but when it comes down to it, a couple weeks of knowing one another does not trusted confidantes make, at least not at times like these.

Perhaps the only time in my life I have ever felt more alone was that day I had the cab come and take me home from the clinic. Justin couldn't be torn away from his lacrosse game with our school's biggest rival. He also couldn't be bothered to come up with the money to help, so I don't know why I was surprised or disappointed.

It had been almost a year since the shit went down. It had started last September, when we returned to boarding school after a summer apart and we could not get our hands off each other. The first time back together we could not even wait long enough to use protection—we didn't care. And the next morning, I knew: trouble. I just felt it. By the beginning of October, I could not deny the changes in my body: sudden cleavage, morning nausea, deepening sense of panic and hysteria that I could share with no one.

I had liked being Justin's girlfriend. I did not want this trouble. I wouldn't say I fooled myself that we were in love— even then, I understood the diff between love and lust, even if the love part I'd yet to experience—but I liked that when I was with Justin, I was Somebody. I was not the weird girl with the unsmiling face and strange mannerisms. I was a pretty girl who people chose on teams and sat with at lunch, the girl hanging on to the varsity jacket of practically the most popular guy at school. I was admired. I could have done without the drugs and alcohol, but those were part of the Justin package, a price I was willing to pay. Believe it, I was the girl I would pass by on the street now and go, "Yuck."

When I told him, the first thing he said was, "But you know I'm planning to, like, go to Princeton. My dad'll kill me over this." Not, "How are *you* doing?" Not, "How are *we* going to take care of this situation?" It was all about him.

The one thing he did do for me was arrange for this girl who was eighteen to lend me her birth certificate. I gave him a picture of me and he got a fake ID made with her name on it. So technically the record states that a certain Allison Fromme, two months past her eighteenth birthday, was the girl who showed up alone at the clinic with a birth certificate and picture ID to back it up and did not need any kind of parental consent to have an unwanted baby torn from her body.

Afterward, the lady at the clinic said, "Is there somebody here to take you home?" and I pointed to a car waiting at the curb outside, which I knew was waiting for a girl who had gone at the same time as me. I said, "There's my ride," and I would have run out, but the cramping in my stomach made it hard even to walk. So I kind of hobbled to the 7-Eleven across the street and called a cab to take me back to school. And may I just say, that was not the first time that cabdriver had picked up a girl from that 7-Eleven and driven her back to that fancy boarding school. You could just tell by the way he kept looking at my pale face in the mirror and asking, "Are you gonna be all right?"

That was the only time I cried, in the back of this stranger's cab, when I realized that the cabdriver was more concerned about me than Justin was.

It's funny to think that Nancy sent me to boarding school thinking that would straighten me out, that I would meet the right people and start to appreciate everything I had been given. And in the end, what had straightened me out and given me hope and life again was going home.

Thirty-six

I think I lay in bed, comatose, for hours. I lost track of time trying to squash down the pain of memories, trying to think about nothing. I finally fell asleep around eight in the evening, and when I awoke at eight the next morning, for all of my twelve hours of sleep, I felt not at all rested. I had tossed and turned the whole night.

Frank came into my room and said, "You doing all right, kiddo?" He held out the telephone to me with his hand over the speaker part. He mouthed the words, "Your mother." I think he was trying to be Mister Cool, giving me the option of shaking my head in case I wanted him to tell her I was still asleep. Somehow, though, the thought of talking to Nancy was not annoying; it was almost comforting.

I took the phone and drowsily said "hi" into it.

I would have thought Nancy would be the drowsy one—it was five in the morning her time. But no, she was all perky morning sunshine. "Guess what!"

I did not say, "That's what!" I said, "Hmm?" So much for our "space."

She said, "I'm here in New York! We flew in last night. We're staying at the Plaza Hotel. Daddy had to come on business for a couple days and I figured I would come too and we could maybe do some shopping together for school clothes for the new school year!"

I think we both knew the shopping for school clothes excuse was a flimsy one to cover up the fact that she simply was incapable of giving me three whole weeks on my own, but I found it curious that, after the previous day's events, I was a little happy to hear Nancy's excited voice. The funny thing was, after dealing with the Justin stuff in the company of people who were my blood but actually felt more like strangers, I kinda missed her.

She said she could have a car waiting downstairs for me in an hour if I could be ready. I said I'd take the subway and meet her in two.

When I got there, she answered the door and threw a giant bear hug around my stiff body. "Hi, sweetie!" she squealed. I don't know how she manages to turn on and turn off like she does. She has the amazing capability to forget all about fights at the drop of a hat, as if Alcatraz and her forbidding me to see Shrimp could be undone just like that, as if, after two and a half weeks in New York and one giant hug, we were at a zero balance, with everything swell and nothing having ever gone wrong to lead us to this point.

Still, I admit, I was glad to see her. And was she ever dressed the part. She was wearing sleek, narrow, white three-quarters pants with a silk navy sleeveless top and white mule sandals over her pale-painted toes, looking lovely and happy to show off her skinny aerobicized body in tasteful, flesh-revealing summer clothing, which you cannot do in the San Francisco summer cold.

"Where's Dad?" I asked. Ash and Josh had stayed in San Fran with Leila and Fernando, which meant they would probably actually behave for a few days, eat normal meals, and go to bed on time.

"He's downstairs in the lounge having a business

meeting. He'll be back up soon to take us to lunch. He can't wait to see you."

We sat down on the plush frilly sofa. "So," she said, "What do you think about Frank?"

I shrugged. "Eh. He's okay." If Nancy felt a moment of triumph, her face did not show it.

She said, "When I talked to him this morning, he said his daughter told him you two ran into Justin yesterday."

My heart rate whizzed back up. I nodded but didn't say anything back.

"He said she thought you were pretty upset afterward."

I felt my body go completely cold and still. That was the only way I would be able to keep it together.

Nancy nudged a little further, as only a mom can do. "Want to talk about it?"

If she hadn't leaned over to smooth my hair back, I might not have fallen apart like I did. But somehow that soft and tender touch from the one person in the world who can make you feel safe and loved, no matter what your differences, set off the tears. I did not outright bawl; no, it was worse; a flood of tears streamed down my face, out of control.

Nancy pulled me to her, surprised. "Honey! I didn't realize it was that bad." She placed my head on her shoulder and stroked my hair. "Tell me, Cyd Charisse. Tell me what happened. What's wrong?"

I couldn't hold it back. I sputtered, "He let me go alone."

"Go where?"

My mouth moved faster than my judgment. "The clinic."

There, I said it. If she was going to punish me or torture

me with another sentence in Alcatraz, so be it.

Instead, she pulled me away a little so she could look me squarely in the eye. Her face was as pale as mine.

She said, "Do you mean what I think you mean?" I nodded. Now it was her eyes that welled with tears. I recoiled a little, thinking she was going to start one of her screaming fits, but instead she grabbed me back to her and kind of rocked me back and forth. We were both crying.

"That little schmuck," she whispered.

After our tears ran their course, we sat together in silence for a few minutes, absorbing the moment, wondering about the consequences of my little secret being out in the open.

When we separated, we were both calm, all cried out. I tell you, I felt better than I had felt in a long time, relieved, lighter, even though I knew she was about to give it to me.

Nancy moved to sit on the ottoman opposite the sofa so she was facing me. Our knees were touching, and she took my hands in hers. She said, "You should have told me. I could have helped you."

"Really?" I said, disbelieving.

"You know, Cyd Charisse, we have our problems. That's normal for a mother and daughter, especially at your age. But no matter what, you are my child, and I am here to help you, to protect you."

"You're not mad?"

"Oh, I'm mad, make no mistake!" She was, too. Her pale face had turned all red and splotchy from the tears and the anger, and her perfect makeup was now streaked on her face. "We'll be dealing with that when you return home and we take a trip to the gynecologist and a family counselor together to talk about these issues. But what's done is done. I can't undo it. I can tell you this. I'm horrified you got into that situation to begin with, but I want you to understand that when it comes to your health and your body, you can never, ever be scared to ask for my help. It's too important. I will always help you and I will always support you."

This was about the last reaction I would have expected from Nancy. Even the thought of having to go to therapy with her did not undo the fact of how cool and understanding she was about the whole deal.

Something clicked. I asked her, "You didn't get any help when you were pregnant with me, did you? Is that why we like hardly ever see your parents in Minnesota or talk to them?"

"Yes," she said. "That has a lot to do with it."

I said, "Did you consider having an abortion when you found out you were pregnant with me?"

I do admire about Nancy that she always tells it straight. She said, "Yes. I even got so far as the abortion clinic. Twice."

"Did Frank go with?"

"Yes."

"How come you didn't?"

"When it came down to it, I just couldn't do it. I knew your father was never going to marry me, knew he was making false promises, I knew he would support me financially, but only in quiet. I knew there was no way I could make it work. But I just couldn't do it. Believe me, I agonized."

"What changed your mind?"

"You might find this shocking, but I had planned to give you up for adoption."

This was shocking. For all that I have not always been the happiest camper in our family, I cannot imagine being part of any other.

"How come you didn't? What changed your mind?"

Nancy said, "My dear, did you ever wonder why you were named for a movie star?"

"Not really," I said. "It's just my name. I thought you named me after that lady because she was your idol."

"She was. But there's another reason. I was all set to give you up for adoption. The papers had been signed, the parents chosen. But I had insisted that I get to name you. I chose the name Cyd Charisse because I wanted to be able to find you, later, and I wanted you to have a name so distinct there could be no mistaking you when I found you. But then, after the birth, they gave you to me to hold, and I couldn't let go. I just couldn't. I knew that whatever it took, I would find a way for us to be together, to be a family."

Just when I thought my tears had run their course, I found a fresh set streaming down my cheeks. I said, "Mom, we don't always get along, but I'm glad you're my mom. I wouldn't want anybody else but you."

She took my hand and rubbed it along her smooth cheek. "That means more to me than anything you could say," she said.

Later, when Sid-dad came back to the hotel room, he found me lying on the sofa, with my head in Nancy's lap. She was stroking my hair and massaging my scalp as I rested. Sid-dad took one look at us then looked up at the room number to make sure he was in the right room.

"Well, aren't you two a sight for sore eyes!" he said.

"Aren't *you!*" I said. I leapt up to give him a hug. "Little hellion," I added.

Nancy went into the bathroom, I think to have a good cry in private.

I sat down with Sid-dad and said, "What was I like as a little girl?"

He said, "Fun, and sweet, and rambunctious and naughty."

"Like Ash and Josh?" I said.

"Yes," he answered. "Just not so loud."

When Nancy had said she knew she would do whatever it took to make us a family, I realized she meant Sid-dad. I told him, "I musta really needed a dad."

Sid-dad gave me one of those looks like in those commercials where the dad sends his daughter off to college and the moment is like so proud and bittersweet at the same time. "You know," he said, "I needed a daughter just as much."

Thirty-seven

On my last evening in New York, after Sid and Nancy had returned to San Francisco, the whole bio-fam Frank clan got together for dinner at a very fancy restaurant. I got to wear my special new-old, perfect-fit dress that belonged to lisBETH and Danny's Grandma Molly (mine too, I guess), and we got to see what we would be like as a real family.

Boring, is the first word that comes to mind.

Lots of, "So, Cyd, what's the first thing you'll do back in San Francisco?" and, "Are you looking forward to going back to school?" You know, the usual deal: lame questions when people really have nothing to say to each other but don't really have anything against each other either, which I guess is something, for this family at least. Watching lisBETH try not to make eyes at Aaron was pretty trippy, and watching Frank try to be discreet checking out all the ladies in fancy dresses and Danny sneak knowing kicks at me under the table, well, it was all cute and good, but my mind was elsewhere: about three thousand miles away in the city where people leave their hearts.

I was busy thinking about my visit with Sid and Nancy, how we had spent a whole day together and not fought, but had talked about the future. Sid didn't get mad when I said I wasn't interested in college and that I wanted to be a barista, at least for a while, maybe own my own café some day, like Java and Danny. I told them really I wouldn't mind skipping out of my senior year of high school entirely and just have a job. Sid-dad said no way, no day, but we did work out a compromise. I will go to school for half a day on a work-study arrangement, and then I will spend three afternoons a week in the business office of his company cafeteria, learning about budgets and inventories, and the other two afternoons volunteering at Sugar Pie's nursing home. We all agreed that if I ended up at junior college, it would not be considered to be a tragedy by any of the relevant parties, but we would revisit the issue after Christmas. Nancy agreed that I can take the bus and not have a driver, but both Sid and Nancy said I cannot tease Fernando about Sugar Pie. Good help is hard to find, they said. Plus, they consider him to be a friend. I said I did too but please not to tell him that because we didn't want his broody head to get too big.

The most interesting part of our day had been when they told me about Shrimp. They said he had come to the house right after I left for New York. They said he'd known from Sugar Pie that I was in New York, and he had come to set the record straight with Sid and Nancy. He said he was sorry and that he accepted full responsibility and that he hoped they wouldn't hold the fact that we were young and stupid against us. Nancy tried not to laugh when she related that last part, and she actually called him "Shrimp" instead of *that boy*. I said does this mean Shrimp and I are off probation, and Nancy said "We'll see," but behind her back, Sid-dad nodded yes.

On the cab ride back from dinner with bio-fam, I asked Frank, could we please stop at Miss Loretta's House of Great Eats. He did not look uncomfortable and said, sure, why not. When we got there, I ran inside and found Miss

Loretta. She pointed to the empty shelf. "You and Gingerbread ready to part ways?" she asked me.

I shook my head. I said, "Naw. Gingerbread is not just a childhood doll. She is as much a part of me as my arms, my legs, my heart. We just wanted to come by and say bye and, like, thanks for the legacy and all."

Miss Loretta twinkle-smiled. "I understand," she said. I think she really did. That is why Gingerbread and I so totally dug Miss Loretta.

Gingerbread and I promised everyone we would make another visit next summer. Danny was the most sad and he said, There'll always be a job here with us for you. Frank said, There will always be a place for you in New York, with us, when you want. I said, Thank you, nice people, and lisBETH said, She really does have good manners, you know?

But by then Gingerbread and I, in our minds, were already halfway home.

Thirty-eight

I thought about it on the plane ride home to San Francisco, my new ultra fantastico tribute commune to all things ginger. Think about it. Sustenance, so long as we keep the ginger roots cultivated, will be easy. We'll live on ginger jerky, ginger chicken, and stirfried ginger veggies, we'll drink ginger ale and ginger beer, and for dessert, oatmeal ginger cookies or our favorite staple, gingerbread.

Ash and Josh will be happy-hyper, because we will put them to work constructing gingerbread houses. We won't care if they eat off the sprinkles and candy hearts that were meant to be decoration, so long as they're careful not to choke. Sid and Nancy will chill on the whole scene because we will serve them ginger tea laced with mellow vibes, and just the thought of all those gingerbread-house colors will keep Nancy occupied, coordinating peppermint-stick patterns and LifeSaver-stained glass windows, and will keep Sid-dad on his toes, worrying about cost overruns and labor laws.

Bio-fam will be invited on special holidays, like Labor Day and Columbus Day, those holidays not meant for intimate family occasions but for overall general ginger barbecue fun. Danny and Aaron will have special ginger-scented permits to come anytime they want, but that will be our secret.

Our slammin' girl Gingerbread will tell Leila RELAX! Gingerbread will run the whole joint. She will decide where the ghosts of Ginger Spice, Ginger Rogers, and Ginger from *Gilligan's Island* are seated at dinner, and she will make all those Gingers help with the cooking and cleaning even if they just did their nails. When Gingerbread is tired of all those Gingers' diva-like antics, Sugar Pie will mosey in to take over. Fernando will make all the ladies swoon with the ginger donuts he will make specially for them.

Once a year we will sponsor a ginger-java marathon run from the Golden Gate Bridge to Ocean Beach. Runners will start out under the red mystical spokes of the bridge with the fog whipping through their bodies, and they will end at the finish line at Java the Hut, where they will be rewarded with caffeine, ginger cookies, and more fog.

At the end of the rainbow in Cyd Charisse's Land of All Things Ginger, there will be a Shrimp.

Author Bio

Rachel Cohn is a graduate of Barnard College and lives in Manhattan. Her first novel, *Gingerbread*, was named to the Best of 2002 lists for *Publishers Weekly*, *School Library Journal*, Barnes & Noble, and the *Bulletin of the Center for Children's Books*, and was a Book Sense 76 pick. Rachel Cohn is also the author of the middle-grade novel *The Steps*, for which she was praised with a starred review in *Publisher's Weekly* for "once again creating a funny and fiesty narrator." Look out for Cohn's next teen novel, *Pop Princess*.

When I was six months old, I dropped from the sky—the lone survivor of a deadly Japanese plane crash. The newspapers named me Heaven. I was adopted by a wealthy family in Tokyo, pampered, and protected. For nineteen years, I thought I was lucky.
I'm learning how wrong I was.

I've lost the person I love most.
I've begun to uncover the truth about my family.
Now I'm being hunted. I must fight back, or die.
The old Heaven is gone.

I AM SAMURAI GIRL.